Totally Joe

Other Books by James Howe

Misfits Novels
The Misfits
Addie on the Inside
Also Known as Elvis

Other Novels
A Night Without Stars
Morgan's Zoo
The Watcher

Edited by James Howe
The Color of Absence: Twelve Stories About Loss and Hope
13: Thirteen Stories That Capture the Agony and Ecstasy of Being Thirteen

Sebastian Barth Mysteries
What Eric Knew
Stage Fright
Eat your Poison, Dear
Dew Drop Dead

Bunnicula Books
Bunnicula (with Deborah Howe)
Howliday Inn
The Celery Stalks at Midnight
Nighty-Nightmare
Return to Howliday Inn
Bunnicula Strikes Again!
Bunnicula Meets Edgar Allan Crow

Tales from the House of Bunnicula
It Came from Beneath the Bed!
Invasion of the Mind Swappers from Asteroid 6!

Howie Monroe and the Doghouse of Doom
Screaming Mummies of the Pharaoh's Tomb II
Bud Barkin, Private Eye
The ~~Amazing~~ Odorous Adventures of Stinky Dog

Bunnicula and Friends
The Vampire Bunny
Hot Fudge
Rabbit-cadabra!
Scared Silly
Creepy-Crawly Birthday
The Fright Before Christmas

Pinky and Rex Series
Pinky and Rex
Pinky and Rex Get Married
Pinky and Rex and the Mean Old Witch
Pinky and Rex and the Spelling Bee
Pinky and Rex Go to Camp
Pinky and Rex and the New Baby
Pinky and Rex and the Double-Dad Weekend
Pinky and Rex and the Bully
Pinky and Rex and the New Neighbors
Pinky and Rex and the Perfect Pumpkin
Pinky and Rex and the School Play
Pinky and Rex and the Just-Right Pet

Picture Books
There's a Monster Under My Bed
There's a Dragon in My Sleeping Bag
Teddy Bear's Scrapbook (with Deborah Howe)
Kaddish for Grandpa in Jesus' Name Amen
Horace and Morris but Mostly Dolores
Horace and Morris Join the Chorus (but what about Dolores?)
Horace and Morris Say Cheese (Which Makes Dolores Sneeze!)

Totally Joe

JAMES HOWE

Atheneum Books for Young Readers
athenenum NEW YORK LONDON TORONTO SYDNEY NEW DELHI

ATHENEUM BOOKS FOR YOUNG READERS
An imprint of Simon & Schuster Children's Publishing Division
1230 Avenue of the Americas, New York, New York 10020
This book is a work of fiction. Any references to historical events, real people, or real locales are used fictitiously. Other names, characters, places, and incidents are products of the author's imagination and any resemblance to actual events or locales or person, living or dead, is entirely conicidental.
Text © 2005 by James Howe
Cover illustration © 2021 by James Bernadin
Cover design © 2021 by Simon & Schuster, Inc.
All rights reserved, including the right of reproduction in whole or in part in any form.
ATHENEUM BOOKS FOR YOUNG READERS is a registered trademark of Simon & Schuster, Inc.
For informaiton about special discounts for bulk purchases, please contact Simon & Schuster Special Sales at 1-866-506-1949 or business@simonandschuster.com.
The Simon & Schuster Speakers Bureau can bring authors to your live event. For more information or to book an event, contact the Simon & Schuster Speakers Bureau at 1-866-248-3049 or visit our website at www.simonspeakers.com.
Also available in an Atheneum Books for Young Readers hardcover edition
Book design by Kristin Smith
The text for this book is set in Jante Antiqua.
Manufactured in the United States of America
0921 OFF
First Atheneum Books for Young Readers paperback edition April 2007
20 19 18 17
The Library of Congress has cataloged the hardcover edition as follows:
Howe, James, 1946–
Totally Joe / by James Howe.—1st ed.
p. cm.
"Ginee Seo Books."
Summary: As a school assignment, a thirteen-year-old boy writes an alphabiography—life from A to Z—and explores issues of friendship, family, school, and the challenges of being a gay teenager.
ISBN 978-0-689-83957-3 (hc)
[1. Gays—Fiction. 2. Schools—Fiction. 3. Friendship—Fiction. 4. Family life—Fiction.]
I. Title.
PZ7H83727 To 2005
[Fic]—dc22 2004022242
ISBN 978-0-689-83958-0 (pbk)

M is for MARK

AND SO IS THIS BOOK. TOTALLY.

Totally Joe

CONFIDENTIAL

To Mr. Daly

(All Other Eyes **KEEP OUT**!)

Dear Mr. Daly,

Okay, I admit it. When you first gave us this assignment,
I thought it was lame. Write about yourself from A-Z?
Bo-ring. (No offense.) Besides worrying that I wouldn't know
what to write for every single letter (Hello, does anybody
know an x-word other than xylophone? And does anybody
play the xylophone? And if they did, would anybody *care*?),
well, I was also thinking, *Can I really tell the truth about
myself?* I'm not ashamed of my life or anything. I'm only
thirteen (twelve, when I started writing this), so I doubt
I've gotten to the *really* embarrassing stuff yet, but,
let's face it, I'm not exactly your average Joe and I get
called plenty of names because of it. And then there was
all the stuff that happened this year. I mean, was I really
going to write about all that? And when you said we had to
end every chapter with a Life Lesson to share with others,
I thought: *Oh. My. God. That is* so *Oprah*.

But I got the point. You wanted us to think. You
wanted this to be *about* something. But if it's about the
real stuff—you know, the truth and all—well, I have
to ask: Mr. Daly, did you think this one through? I mean,
hello, we're in the seventh grade. Every single thing
anybody knows about us is ammunition. And have you
thought about the fact that we would end up talking about
other people in our "alphabiographies," as you call them?
I mean, we could be sued for *libel*. I know about this stuff.
I watch Court TV.

Well, anyway, here it is. I started it in October and
finished it last week. You're the first person to read it—
other than me, I mean. I haven't even shown it to my
best friends, who all shared what they wrote and were, like,
"We're never speaking to you again" when I wouldn't let
them read what I wrote—especially Addie, who doesn't
know the meaning of "It's none of your business." Well,
actually, Bobby was okay with my not sharing. He respects
privacy. But the others were, like, "Joe, it's not like we
don't know everything about you, anyway." But the thing is,
I wrote stuff in here that I've never written down before.
Some of it I didn't even *know* until I wrote it down.
It's kind of personal (and some of it is seriously private).
I had to decide if I should take some stuff out before

handing it in, but I liked writing it and it's all the truth—
and that's what you said we should go for, right?

But the thing is, Mr. Daly, if you wouldn't mind keeping
what I've written to yourself, that would be okay with me.
Really. Whatever you do, *please* don't ask me to read any
of it in front of the class, even if you think it's the best
alphabiography you've ever read. I mean, I wouldn't want
to betray other people—and the thing with my mother's
high heels is not something I need everybody to know about.
Ammunition, remember?

Yours truly,

Joe (formerly JoDan) Bunch

OCTOBER

A is for

ADDIE

IT MIGHT SEEM FUNNY TO START AN AUTOBIOGRAPHY BY WRITING ABOUT somebody else, but there's a simple reason: Addie is one of my first memories.

I was four years old when I moved to Paintbrush Falls, right next door to this tall, skinny girl named Addie Carle. I found out later her real name was Addison. I made that number six on the "Weird Things About Our Neighbors" list I had going in my head. I remember the list:

1. These people don't eat meat. Not even hot dogs. They eat something called Tofu Pups instead. (Gross.)
2. The mother doesn't shave her armpits. (Gross.)
3. The father likes to be called by his first name. (Graham.)
4. The girl (Addie) is my age and knows how to read. Or *says* she does.

5. Addie thinks my favorite movie star has a stupid name and that there must be something wrong with her.

6. Addie's real name is Addison, which is a lot stupider than Cher, and I think there must be something wrong with *her*.

In case you're wondering, I had never seen Cher in a movie. I was only four. But I had seen her on an infomercial once, and, I don't know, it's like we instantly bonded. This is something that Addie, to this day, does not get. I love Addie—as a friend—but she can be *so* dense. Honestly.

So here's what I remember: this tall, skinny girl picking her nose while eating a peanut butter sandwich. It's not pretty, but I can't help what my first memories are, can I? And think about it: Wouldn't that make an impression on *you*?

She was sitting on her front-porch steps. I walked over and stared at her picking her nose and eating her sandwich. Finally she said, "I thought you were supposed to be a boy. Why are you wearing a dress?" I told her that that was for me to know and her to find out. She said, "Oh, I will." Then she offered me a bite of her sandwich, but because of the booger factor, I politely said no. I think we went up to her room after that and played with her Legos.

Oh, I just remembered something else weird. It might have been #4½ on my list. Addie did not have any Barbies. I mean, what kind of girl doesn't have *any* Barbies? I was only four and not even a girl, and I had seven Barbies, at least.

The no-Barbies thing made me feel sorry for Addie for a while, but then I started to think that even without Barbies she was the luckiest person in the world. Why? Because she's an only child! I couldn't believe it when I found out. I was, like, "You're soooo lucky!" And she was, like, "Nuh-uh, you're luckier. You have a big brother." Please. She had no idea what it was like having a brother who was totally different from you. I mean, Jeff is nice and all, but he's this total guy-guy who's all "yo" and "dude" and grabbing at his crotch and belching. (I don't mean to be crude, but, honestly, that's how it is.) Of course, when we were younger, Jeff wasn't like that so much. But, still, he was always into sports big-time, while me, all I have to do is *see* a ball and I get a nosebleed.

It's funny. Even though we're so different—and whatever the opposite of guy-guy is, that's what *I* am—Jeff has never made fun of me. Even when I was going through my Easy-Bake oven stage (which lasted from my sixth birthday until the unfortunate incident with the lasagna when I was seven), he'd come home all sweaty from playing football or something and find me in an apron making cookies, and he wouldn't say anything nasty like, "Nice apron, Martha Stewart." The worst he'd do was grab a cookie and belch. Even when he was with his friends, he pretty much left me alone. (Except for grabbing cookies.)

The point is, once we moved to Paintbrush Falls, Jeff and I never played together, which was okay with me because I had Addie next door to play with, and right off the bat Addie introduced me to her best friend, Bobby Goodspeed.

Addie is really smart, as everybody at Paintbrush Falls Middle School knows. (I mean, it's hard *not* to know, when she's in your face about it 24/7.) But her being smart can be a good thing. Like when we first met, after she asked me about the dress and after I asked her to come over to my house to play Barbies and she said, "*You* have Barbies?" she pretty much had me figured out and stopped asking questions. I think it helped that she *loved* playing Barbies. Her parents were so *anti*-Barbie they probably would have sent her off to boarding school if they'd ever found out what was going on next door. Needless to say, she never told them. (I seem to recall that Addie liked Teacher Barbie best, which if you know Addie, will totally not be a surprise.)

Still, over the years Addie's smarts have gotten her into all kinds of trouble. Like what's going on right now, with her refusing to say the Pledge of Allegiance because she says we don't have liberty and justice for all in this country and she doesn't like making empty pledges. I'm not sure how I feel about what she's doing. I mean, I respect her for standing up for what she believes in (and I kind of agree with her about it)—and it's totally cool that she and Bobby have gotten everybody in school talking about name-calling—but, I don't know, I've got to be honest: Sometimes I wish she'd just shut up and sit down.

She would *so* kill me if she knew I felt that way.

So why do I feel that way? I guess it's because when you're a boy like me, you kind of get noticed all the time. You don't need to have a friend who is always opening her big mouth and bringing even more attention your way. At the same time, Addie has always stood up for me. She's never been afraid to tell Kevin Hennessey off when he's called me names or tripped me or yanked my hair. I never thought about it before, but it was probably because of Addie that I learned how to tell Kevin Hennessey off myself. (Not that I always do. But at least I know the words I would say if I had the nerve to say them.)

LIFE LESSON: Standing up for other people can help them learn to stand up for themselves.☺

☺ Mr. Daly: I was going to say, "Don't pick your nose and eat a peanut-butter sandwich at the same time," but I have a feeling this is more what you had in mind. Am I right?

B is for
BOY

TODAY IN GYM KEVIN HENNESSEY CALLED ME
A GIRL. I REMINDED HIM THAT WE'RE TRYING TO
stop name-calling in our school, and he said, "I'm not
calling you a name, faggot, I'm calling you a girl, which you
are." I didn't even bother to point out that "faggot" is a
name. *What* is the point? Kevin Hennessey has an IQ
smaller than his neck size. Actually, he has a *head* smaller
than his neck size. I'm so not kidding.

Well, I'm used to being called a girl, but, *excuse* me, is
that supposed to be an insult? What's wrong with girls?
Some of my best friends are girls! But I know what Kevin
H. and all the other (um, no name-calling, so you'll have
to use your imagination here) _____s mean when they
say it. They mean I'm not a boy.

Okay, fine, I'm not a boy like *them*, but I'm still a boy.
The thing is, boys—by which I mean guy-guys like my
brother, Jeff—have always been a total mystery to me. I
mean, how do they know how to do all that stuff, like

throw and catch and grease car engines? Besides the fact that I don't have a clue how to do any of those things, on a scale of 1-10 I have, like, below zero interest. *Way* below. Try negative a thousand.

But when you're a boy, people just expect you to:

1. Make fart noises under your armpit and think it's hilarious.
2. Make *real* farts and go, "Good one!"
3. Spit.
4. Relate to other boys by punching and shoving and calling them "jerk" and "butthead" and other names I'd better not put down if I want a good grade. (Guy-guy Fact: Calling somebody "butthead"—or worse—is considered even more brilliantly hilarious than making armpit noises.)
5. Relate to girls by teasing or ignoring them. (Except when you're with other boys, and then you brag about all the things you've done with girls, even if you've never really done any of them and would probably pass out if you actually had the chance to *kiss* a girl.)
6. Wave your hand around in class all the time until the teacher finally calls on you and then say, "I forgot."

7. Laugh at the other boys who wave their hands around in class all the time until the teacher finally calls on them and they say, "I forgot."

8. Be an expert on
   a. video games
   b. cars
   c. sports
   d. fixing things
   e. acting tough

9. Act tough.

10. Use the word "faggot" at least twenty times a day.

If they didn't spend so much time trying to make my life miserable (at least fifteen out of every twenty "faggots" are guaranteed to be directed at boys like me), I'd actually feel sorry for guy-guys. I mean, they must get so tired of having to spit and fart and act tough all the time.

Okay, here's the part that's hard for me to admit: As much as I don't understand guy-guys—and sometimes actually feel sorry for them—I went through a period in my life when I wanted to *be* one. I kept thinking there was something wrong with me for not knowing how to, I don't know, be a boy. It's just so natural for Jeff to want to play football and know how to do it and enjoy watching it on TV. Sometimes Jeff and his friends are talking about some game, and it's like they are speaking a foreign language. *C'est vrai!* (Culture Note: That means "It's true!" in French.)

The worst is on Thanksgiving, when we have all these relatives over and the guy-guys are down in the basement watching the Super Bowl or whatever it is that's on TV on Thanksgiving (and what a football game has to do with Pilgrims and Native Americans is beyond me) (unless maybe at the first Thanksgiving the turkey got overcooked and the Pilgrims tossed it to the Native Americans and that's how football was invented) (just a guess), and I'm in the kitchen with my mom and Aunt Pam and all the other female members of the family, and I keep thinking I should be down in the basement watching the game, but I don't want to because I would shrivel up and die from boredom, and, anyway, I don't speak the language. I do, however, speak "kitchen" fluently.

Luckily, I have two best friends—Bobby Goodspeed and Skeezie Tookis—who are guys but not guy-guys.

I also have Colin (see C).

Bobby and Skeezie have been my friends for years. Still, even with them as best friends (along with Addie), it hasn't always been easy. I don't know why, but all of a sudden in the fifth grade I wanted to be a guy-guy so badly that I actually asked Skeezie to teach me how. Oh. My. God. It was pathetic.

Skeezie: Stop crossing your legs at the knee.

Me: What does that have to do with being a guy-guy?

Skeezie: It has to do with guys do not cross their legs at the knee. Your aunt Priscilla crosses her legs at the knee.

Me: I don't have an aunt Priscilla. Although I wish I did. I *love* the name.

Skeezie: *You're* an aunt Priscilla, okay? Now, listen up and do what I'm tellin' ya. If you gotta cross your legs, you keep one leg at a right angle to the floor and put your other ankle on the knee of that leg. Like this.

Me: Oh my god, you look just like that gangster in that movie. You know, the one with Al Pacino and all the blood? We saw it at Bobby's that time.

Skeezie: Do it, lame brain.

Me: Ow. It hurts.

Skeezie: Stop waving your hands around.

Me: I'm not waving—

Skeezie: Yes, you are. Guys don't wave their hands around. They keep their hands quiet.

Me: Well, *that's* boring.

Skeezie: What are you doing?

Me: What?

Skeezie: Your hands. You're folding them in your lap.

Me: I'm keeping them quiet.

Skeezie: Your aunt Priscilla sits with her hands folded in her lap.

Me: Not with her legs crossed like this, she doesn't. Where are you going?

Skeezie: I give up. Just be who you are, okay?

Me: But you haven't taught me how to talk sports yet. So, what do you think about those Yankees? Huh, Skeezie? Huh? How 'bout them Yankees?

Skeezie never did teach me how to talk sports. And I never stopped crossing my legs at the knee. When you come right down to it, I'm a lot more comfortable sitting like my aunt Priscilla than like a gangster in some movie I can't even remember the name of.

I wish I *did* have an aunt Priscilla.

LIFE LESSON: Just be who you are, okay?

C is for
COLIN

OKAY, THIS IS REALLY FUNNY. ONE OF THE FIRST THINGS COLIN TOLD ME THIS YEAR (actually, he wrote it in this note he put in my locker) (which at first I thought was from somebody else since it was unsigned) (and why in the *universe* would Colin Briggs be putting a note in *my* locker?) was: "I wish I could be like you."

That's funny, right? Correction: That's hilarious. Me! He wanted to be like *me. Nobody* wants to be like Joe Bunch, and who wouldn't want to be like Colin Briggs? He is:

1. Totally cool.
2. Smart.
3. A jock.
4. Really nice.
5. To everybody, even if they're *not* totally cool, smart, a jock, really nice, or popular.

6. Popular.
7. Cute.
8. *Seriously* cute.
9. Especially when he smiles.

In other words, we had, like, zero in common. But then I found out last Thursday that we *did* have something in common. And now (drumroll, please): COLIN BRIGGS IS MY BOYFRIEND!

I can't believe I just wrote that. I probably should have written: Colin Briggs is my boyfriend. But I want to shout it. I mean, I have had this major crush on Colin Briggs since fifth grade. (Fifth grade was a big year for me, figuring-out-who-I-was-wise.) And now he's my *boyfriend*—and all because I'm not afraid to be myself, and he likes that!

Still, I'm a little worried about what Kevin Hennessey might do if he saw this declaration of boyfriendship in writing. Picture it: I'm walking down the hall, and Kevin grabs my notebook and tears it open and yells so the whole school can hear (because he really doesn't know the meaning of "indoor voice"): "Hey, get this—Colin and Joseph*ine* are *boy*friends! Ooo, we always knew you were a faggot, Bunch, but didja have to turn Briggs into one, too? Youse two are disgusting!" Okay, so he probably wouldn't say "youse two." I mean, we live in Paintbrush Falls, New York, in the twenty-first century, not Brooklyn in the 1940s. (I have been watching *way* too many old movies with Bobby.) But that doesn't mean he wouldn't do something really . . . well, I don't know what he'd do, but it would probably involve pain.

I was almost sure he'd figured it out on Friday when Colin and I were at the school dance together. Of course, no one knew we were "together." We were with our friends the whole time, but it *was* unusual for our groups to be mixing. I mean, Colin and I had never spent any time in school hanging out together before then, unless you want to count our being seated near each other because of our last names: Briggs and Bunch.

Kevin and that _____ (fill in the blank) Jimmy Lemon noticed us right away and kept coming over and making little kissy noises.

Finally, Kevin said, "You girls gonna dance together?"

I came back with, "Why don't you and Jimmy show us how?"

Jimmy Lemon laughed at that. I think mainly because he wasn't smart enough to have figured out what I was saying. But Kevin didn't like it at all. He turned to Colin and said, "You better watch out, Briggs. You hang out with queers, you end up with—"

Skeezie cut him off and said, "A fabulous eye for color?"

"Hardy-har, greaseball," Kevin retorted.☺ (It seems like Kevin must have slept through the assembly the day before when Bobby gave this big student council campaign speech against name-calling, which everybody in the whole school thought was awesome.) (Except, obviously, Kevin.)

"What I was going to say was, if you hang out with queers, people might think *you're* a queer."

Colin turned white. I mean, whiter than usual, since he has this really fair complexion. I thought, *Well, it's been nice having a boyfriend for, let's see, thirty-two hours and forty-seven minutes,* figuring, you know, that he wasn't going to be able to take the heat, and probably the minute Kevin walked away, he'd tell me it was nice knowing me and see you around.

But then before Skeezie or any of the rest of us could think what to say, Colin blurted out, "You and Jimmy have been trying to hang out with us since we got here, Kevin. I wonder what people are saying about *you.*"

That was so funny. I almost hugged Colin. (Except of

☺ Mr. D: Do I get extra points for words like "retorted"?

course I wouldn't have with Kevin and Jimmy standing there.) (Besides which, Colin and I hadn't hugged each other *ever*, and it was so not going to happen for the first time at a school dance.)

It did make Kevin Hennessey leave us alone for the rest of the evening, though. And when I asked Colin later if he was worried about what Kevin thought, he just said, "No," in that quiet way of his, and I felt sure I'd have a boyfriend for a lot longer than thirty-two hours and whatever minutes.

Did you ever have a dream you thought could never come true? I mean, it just seemed totally impossible? Like walking into the Candy Kitchen to get an ice cream soda and . . . Oh. My. God. Isn't that *Julia Roberts* sitting at the counter? And she's waving you over! And you spend the whole rest of the day hanging out with her, laughing, and . . . well, Colin being my boyfriend seemed even more impossible than that!

My crush on Colin Briggs started the first time I saw him two years ago. He had just moved here from Someplace, Ohio. Mrs. Kubrich introduced him to our class and then asked me to move back a desk and asked Colin to take my old seat. I couldn't believe it! He was sitting right in front of me! I spent the entire rest of the day looking at the back of his head and thinking . . . well, to be honest, I was thinking that the back of his head was shaped like a melon, which is probably what everybody's head is shaped like, but we had just had melon for dessert the night before and I had made such a production out of telling my mother that I hated melon that, well, now it was deeply disturbing to find myself falling in love with someone whose head kept reminding me of a fruit I had taken a stand on *never eating even if it was the last edible substance on the face of the planet,* like, just fifteen hours earlier. Of course, melons don't have feathery blond hair. And Colin's head did. So that helped.

When I wasn't thinking about how much I hated melons or how much I liked Colin's hair, I was trying to figure out what I would say to him after the bell rang. I thought maybe I'd say something about cleaning out my old desk, which was now *his* desk, but that was so lame. Then I thought I'd ask if he wanted to have lunch with me, and then I remembered where I actually sat in the cafeteria, and I thought maybe it would be insulting to ask him to sit with the least popular kids in the entire school. By the time the bell rang, I hadn't thought of anything better than, "I like your head, even if it *is* shaped like a melon." Fortunately, I was saved from the death sentence of saying that out loud because Drew Geller came right over to him and said, "Come on, Colin, I'll show you where the cafeteria is. You can eat at our table."

I hated how Drew said the word "our." Like: "We're the best." But I couldn't really hate Drew, because he probably didn't mean it that way. Drew is nice, even if he is popular, and I knew at that moment that Colin was going to be popular, too. I decided then and there that I should be grateful to have a one-sided relationship with the back of Colin's head and not hope for anything more.

For the rest of fifth grade and all of sixth, Colin and I said maybe fifty words to each other. I wrote his initials maybe five hundred times. And I stared at the back of his head maybe a thousand. (I sat behind him all through fifth grade and in two classes in sixth.) I never, ever, *ever* imagined that he would like me the way I liked him, and I hated myself for liking him the way I did.

"Why can't I like girls?" I asked Bobby once. He was the only one of my friends I could tell about Colin and know that a) he would understand, and b) he would keep it a secret.

"Have you ever *tried* to like girls?" Bobby asked. It was the night before my eleventh birthday party. I had just gone through three weeks of stomachaches trying to decide whether or not to invite Colin, knowing the whole time there was no way I would.

"Sure," I told him. "I imagined myself married to Julia Roberts once, but all we did was talk about her clothes. I don't think my father has ever had a conversation with my mother about her clothes, except to go, 'Uh-huh,' when she asks him if he likes her new sweater or something. So I figured I wasn't really the marrying kind."

Bobby just shook his head. "I'm not a good person to ask about this," he said. "I don't think I'm ever going to get married or even like anybody. I can't imagine it. I'll live alone. I might have a dog."

"Dogs are nice," I said. "Maybe I'll get a dog and name it Colin. Because dogs love you back, right?"

Bobby is a good friend. He didn't laugh at me when I said that. Instead, he asked me what kind of dog I would get, but all I could think to say was that it would have to have blond hair and a head shaped like a melon.

My party was on Saturday. It was pretty good. My aunt Pam, who had moved in with us a few weeks before, baked this amazing cake that looked like the *Titanic* just before it went under. (I was in my *Titanic* phase.) But what I remember most is the wish I made when I blew out the candles. I thought, *Well, this is a waste of a perfectly good wish*, but I couldn't help myself.

On Monday, a mini-miracle happened. Colin turned around while Mrs. Kubrich was writing some vocabulary words on the board and said, "Happy birthday." (Monday was my actual birthday.)

I said, "How did you know?"

He said, "Oh, a little bird told me."

I never found out who the little bird was, because Mrs. Kubrich said whoever was talking had better stop, and Colin turned back around.

Up until last week, Colin wishing me a happy birthday was just about the best thing that had ever happened in my whole life. And then last Thursday he told me he liked me, and it turned out my eleventh-birthday wish hadn't been wasted at all.

LIFE LESSON: There's no such thing as a wasted wish.

D is for
DATING

TWO WEEKS AGO, ME AND MY FRIENDS—
ADDIE, BOBBY, AND SKEEZIE—WERE ALL

single. Now—except for Skeezie, who is Mr. Don't-Talk-To-Me-About-Love-It-Makes-Me-Want-To-Puke, even though we all *know* he has a thing for one of the waitresses at the Candy Kitchen (WHO IS OLD ENOUGH TO BE HIS OLDER SISTER, BY THE WAY!)—we're all dating. I am soooo excited—and also, at the same time, confused.

Addie is going out with DuShawn. Bobby (who thought he would never like anybody, remember?) is going out with Kelsey. And I'm going out with Colin. But everybody knows that Addie is going out with DuShawn and that Bobby is going out with Kelsey. And Colin and me, well, we're kind of in the closet. What I mean is, Addie and DuShawn have already been seen holding hands in the halls, so of course everyone is talking about them. And Bobby and Kelsey are always blushing around each other, which is *so* Disney

Channel. If I hear one more person say how cute they are . . . well, I'll probably nod and go, "Uh-huh," because, I'm sorry, they *are* cute. It's just that I want people to think Colin and I are cute, too, and I want to hold hands in the halls.

(Seventh-Grade Reality Check: You are two boys. Hello. No one is going to think you're cute. At best, they'll go, "Ick." At worst . . . well, let's not go there, okay?)

So what is the point of dating if we have to keep it a big fat secret?

Are we even dating?

Our three big conversations so far:

Conversation #1

Where: Out by the flagpole

When: Last Thursday after school

The first part: Blah blah um er how's it going blah blah blah

The important part:

Colin: There's something I want to tell you. I, um, like you.

Me: Really? I, um, like you, too.

Colin: I have since last year.

Me: Really? I've liked you since fifth grade.

Colin: Really?

A looooooooong pause.

Colin: Do you want to, you know, go out?

Me: Go out?

Colin: I mean, we don't have to, if . . .

Me: No, I mean, yes, I want to.

Colin: Okay.

Me: Okay. So I guess we're going out, then.

Colin: Right.

Me: Okay.

Colin: Sweet.

Me: Excellent.

Conversation #2

Where: On the phone

When: Thursday evening, three hours and twenty minutes
after Conversation #1

Colin: Hi, it's Colin.

Me: Oh, hi. So, what're you doing?

Colin: Calling you. What're *you* doing?

Me: Being called.

Colin *(laughing)*: You're funny.

Me: No, I'm funny when I'm not nervous. Right now,
I'm nervous. When I'm nervous, all I am is nervous. And
fairly stupid. And I talk too much.

Colin: Well, I'm nervous, too.

Me: Really?

Colin: Sure. I never called a boy before. I mean . . . well, you know what I mean.

Me: Uh-huh, I know. Did you ever call a girl before?

Colin: Once. My mom made me.

Me: She *made* you? That is so *Mommie Dearest*!

Colin: Huh?

Me: *Mommie Dearest*. It's an old movie about this real witch of a mother. I saw it over at Bobby's. He's into old movies. Oh, not that your mother is a witch, I mean . . . I'm not saying that, I mean, I don't even *know* your mother. Did you ever hear of Joan Crawford?

Colin: No.

Me: She was a movie star in the olden days. Only, this movie isn't *with* her, it's *about* her. And all the horrible things she did to her daughter in real life. It's totally over the top. Do you like movies?

Colin: Sure. Have you seen all the Matrix movies? They're awesome.

Me: I saw the first one. Keanu Reeves is so hot.

Colin: Um.

Me: Well, isn't he?

Colin: I guess. I never really thought about it.

Me: Oh. So who's your favorite movie star?

Colin: I don't have one.

Me: Get *out*! You don't have a favorite movie star?

Colin: Is that bad?

Me: Yeah-huh. But don't worry about it, help is on its way. Ta-da!

Colin: What about baseball? Are you watching the play-offs?

Me *(cursing Skeezie for not teaching me how to talk sports)*: Well, I haven't . . . really . . . had . . . time. I've been so busy with, you know . . .

Colin *(laughing this seriously cute laugh)*: It's okay. You're not into sports. I'm cool with that.

Me: Honest? Well, I'm cool with you not having a favorite movie star.

Colin: Honest?

Me: Semi-honest.

Colin: Oh. So, do you want to see a movie Saturday? Maybe I'll find a favorite star.

Me: Okay. We could watch the play-thingies, too. If you want to.

Colin: Play-offs. And that's okay, we don't have to. Well, I'd better go. I still have all that French homework.

Me: *Moi, aussi.*☺ But wait, Colin . . .

Colin: Yeah?

☺ French for "Me, too."

Me: Um, Skeezie and Bobby and Addie and me, we're going to the dance tomorrow night, and I was wondering if . . . I mean, you probably want to go with Drew and your other friends, but . . .

Colin: Why don't we all go together? I mean, you and me, we're . . . you know . . .

Me: Oh, good. I was afraid maybe you changed your mind.

Colin: What? No way!

Me: Good. So we'll go together. Well, I'll see you in school tomorrow. Good luck with the election.

Colin: You, too. And we'll see each other Saturday, too. Right?

Me: Saturday?

Colin: The movies, remember?

Me: Oh, right. I told you, I get a little stupid sometimes.

Conversation #3

Where: Colin's house

When: Saturday, after going to the movies and having dinner with his family

The first part: blah blah the movie blah blah your parents are really nice blah and your little sister is so cute and this is a cool room blah blah blah

The important part:

Me: So right now I like to be called JoDan. That's a combination of my first and middle names. Joseph and Daniel. My parents are *so* unimaginative. With a last name like Bunch, the least they could have done is named me *Alain*—that's French for Alan—or Keanu or something. Lately, I've been thinking of calling myself Soleil or maybe Jade. Soleil might be a tad pretentious, but I like Jade. It keeps the J and d thing going. But I still like JoDan, too. I don't know, what do you think?

Colin: I think you should be happy with Joe.

Me: Really? *You* have such a cool name. Colin. It's like a character in a novel. But Joe. Ugh.

A loooooooong pause.

Me: I'm sorry. I'm talking too much.

Colin: It's okay. And, anyway, you're not talking too much. I was just thinking . . . Joe, I mean, JoDan . . .

Me: You can call me Joe.

Colin: Joe. I was thinking about Kevin and Jimmy at the dance last night. And the way my father was . . .

Me: What?

Colin: Looking at us during dinner. Do you think he knows?

Me: I think he was mostly looking at me. I'll bet your

other friends don't have streaked hair or painted pinky fingernails.

Colin *(laughing)*: You're right about that. I just . . . I don't think I'm ready for my parents to know about us. About me. I thought this was going to be easier. It took me a whole year to work up the nerve to tell you, and now that I have . . .

Me: It's okay. It can be our thing. Nobody else has to know.

Colin: That would be okay with you?

Me: Semi-okay.

Colin: Oh.

Me: No, I mean it's okay. Honest. But what if somebody asks?

Colin: I don't know. Act like we don't know what they're talking about?

Me: Great. Don't ask, don't tell.

Colin: It's not anybody's business, anyway. The important thing is, we can still do stuff together, hang out—even in school—just not like . . .

Me: Just not like . . . boyfriends.

Colin: Not like boyfriends out in the open for everybody to see. Okay?

Me: It's okay. Your dad seems nice, though. He's not going to suddenly hate you if he does find out.

Colin: I wouldn't be so sure about that. What about your parents?

Me: We've never talked about it, but I think they know. And I'm pretty sure they're okay with letting me be whoever I am.

Colin: You are so lucky.

Me: That's what my aunt Pam keeps telling me.

Colin: She's right.

When my dad picked me up from Colin's house Saturday, I was quiet the whole way home. Quiet is not exactly my thing, so my dad started asking all these questions. Was I okay? Did something happen at Colin's? Did I need to talk about anything?

I just kept shaking my head, but inside I was, like, screaming, *Yes! I want to talk about everything! I want to tell you and the whole world that Colin is my boyfriend, and I want you and the whole world to say, "That's great!" Or maybe I want you and the whole world to not even care because it's no big deal. Because it should be no big deal. But it is, and that's why Colin is afraid and why we're going out but nobody knows.*

Finally, my dad said, "Whenever you want to talk, I'm here."

I almost blurted out everything then, but this big lump came into my throat and I knew if I tried to speak all I'd do is end up crying.

LIFE LESSON: "Don't ask, don't tell" sucks!

E is for
E.T.

OKAY, CONFESSION: MY FAVORITE MOVIE IS NOT
THE WIZARD OF OZ (WHICH I READ SOMEWHERE IS
supposed to be, like, *the* gay movie or something) (I have no idea why) or anything with Keanu Reeves or Leonardo DiCaprio (even if they do have fabulous names and are majorly cute). My fave movie is *E.T.—the Extra-Terrestrial.* Unlike Keanu Reeves or Leonardo DiCaprio, E.T. does not have a fabulous name and is majorly *ugly,* but ever since the first time I saw him (I was six), I couldn't get him out of my mind. I began thinking I was from some other planet and wishing I could go home, just like E.T.☺ I would even look up at the sky at night and try to pick out which planet was mine. I had a name for it—Wisteria.

I think that's really the name of a flower or a perfume or something, but I liked the sound of it. I never told anybody, not Bobby or my aunt Pam or anybody. Wisteria was just for me.

☺ Mr. D: Don't worry. I didn't *really* believe I was from some other planet.

I never pictured Wisteria very clearly in my mind. I didn't know what the houses looked like or the trees or people or anything. When I imagined myself living there, it wasn't what I saw that mattered. It was what I felt. I felt at home.

Is that totally weird or what?

Because I love my family and they love me. And I have really good friends who would probably cry even harder than Elliott if I ever *really* went off to some other planet. But sometimes I get this feeling like I'm far from home. Like, I could be sitting with my family watching TV or hanging out with my friends at the Candy Kitchen, and this feeling will come over me, like: *What am I doing here? I don't belong.*

Oh, and remember those scientists who practically kill E.T.? Well, there aren't any scientists after me, but there *is* Kevin Hennessey. Sometimes I think Kevin would kill me if he could get away with it. Honestly. I don't know why he hates me so much. Yesterday, he shoved me up against my locker and called me a totally disgusting name, which I *so* cannot write down here. I mean it. I was going to tell him, "Takes one to know one," but sanity kicked in and I kept my mouth shut. The way his face was all red and twisted, I swear he might have started punching me out any minute.

On Wisteria there are no Kevin Hennesseys.

I was so glad it was Friday. That meant two days without Kevin and at least one *with* Colin. Colin and I have spent time together every weekend for the past three weeks. I've even gone to his cross-country meets.☺ And he's come over to my house to watch movies. We haven't talked any more about being boyfriends. We just kind of know it's there.

Anyway, we didn't have any plans to hang out last night, but I was feeling so bad because of the whole Kevin thing that I called Colin and asked if he wanted to come over after dinner. He did, and the best thing happened! You're never going to believe it, not in a million years!

There he was, standing in the doorway with this DVD in his hand. He said, "I still don't have a favorite movie star, but I do have a favorite movie."

He showed me, and I said, "Oh. My. God. It's *E.T.*!"

He said, "Oh. My. God. Yes, it is!" (That's Colin trying to sound like me.) (Which was *so* funny.) (I guess you had to be there.)

Well, anyway, we went down to the basement and watched the movie, just the two of us. Jeff was up in his bedroom glued to his computer. Dad started watching

---

☺ Look who's talking sports! (Okay, I admit I called them "games" until he told me what they were really called, but still.)

with us, but Mom and Aunt Pam got him to go upstairs. So it was just me and Colin, watching our favorite movie, saying our favorite lines together, cracking up when Drew Barrymore starts screaming her head off the first time she sees E.T. And at the end, when they're saying goodbye and E.T. touches Elliott's head with his finger, Colin reached over and touched my head and said right along with E.T. in this, like, *perfect* E.T. voice, "I'll be right here."

I told him, "That was awesome," meaning the voice. But all I could think about was his finger touching my head. I totally thought I'd died and gone to heaven.

No. It was better than that.

I thought I'd gone to Wisteria.

LIFE LESSON: You don't have to travel to some other planet to find your way home.

F is for
FAMILY
MY FRIENDS ALL THINK MY FAMILY IS
SOOOO COOL. ESPECIALLY MY PARENTS

and Aunt Pam. It's not that they don't think Jeff is cool. He's just not on their radar screens. Okay, it's true Addie had a crush on him once when she was younger, but then she decided that having the hots for your friend's older brother (who also happens to be a jock and not exactly what you'd call politically enlightened) was too much for her feminist soul, so she went from giggling whenever he was around to making these *huh* noises to pretty much ignoring him.

So, anyway, this is who is in my family:

I'll start with Jeff because I've already written about him and there's not much else to say. He is:

1. 15
2. Growing what he calls a beard.☺

☺ It is physically impossible not to laugh when he says this.

3. Obsessed with a girl he met at camp last summer whose name is something that ends in *na* (Joanna, Sienna, Brianna, Banana, whatever). He mostly calls her Clark, which I believe is her last name. She calls him "the J-man." This is so *not* a healthy relationship.

   (Guy-guy Fact: Guy-guys love putting "the" in front of their names and adding "man," "ski," or "ster" after them, as in: "the J-man," "the Jeffski," "the Jeffster.")

4. An expert on all those guy-guy things I talked about back in B. (Except acting tough. As I said before, despite everything, he's actually a fairly decent human being.)

5. Possibly a computer genius (*definitely* a computer geek).

6. The owner of a stunningly boring wardrobe, made up of two colors and the World's Largest Collection of Identical Pairs of Athletic Shoes.

7. The quietest member of our family.

In some ways he and my dad are alike. They both love sports, they're both into their computers, and they both have beards (except my dad's actually *is* a beard). Oh, and they both love these meat-snacky things called Slim Jims. Do not ask. I am, like, *this* close to becoming a vegetarian.

But in other ways my dad is like me. We're both funny (well, *I* think I'm funny, thank you very much), we both like to talk (although we often talk about different things; my father has nothing to say about hair, clothes, or movie stars), and we both like to cook.

My dad's name is David, but everybody calls him Dave. He's a social worker at this agency over in Saratoga that works with "troubled teens." My dad loves kids, and it's pretty obvious to anybody with eyes that he loves Jeff and me. He's always outside with Jeff throwing a ball around or shooting baskets. When they're inside, he gets Jeff to help him with computer stuff. With me, he plays games and watches movies (he gets a little squirmy during chick flicks like *Steel Magnolias*,☺ but he hangs in there), and, as I said, we both like to cook, so sometimes it'll just be the two of us out in the kitchen making dinner for the family.

The best thing about my dad is that he's not afraid of showing what he feels. He's big on hugs (even with my friends, which is one reason they like him so much) and . . . Oh. My. God . . . he cries at the drop of a hat! True story: Last Christmas, Bobby and I were watching

---

☺ #3 on my current Top Ten List, after *E.T.* and *Titanic*.

A Christmas Carol—the old one in black-and-white—and my dad happens to walk through the room right at the moment when Tiny Tim says, "God bless us, every one," and he starts sniffling!

"Dad," I say, "are you *crying?*"

And he's all choking back these tears and he says, "Gets me every time."

Maybe you don't think that's a cool thing in a dad, but I do. Colin says my dad is THE BEST and that I shouldn't worry about telling him I'm gay. He's right. I don't know why I *do* worry about it. Maybe it's because when I see Dad and Jeff outside shooting baskets, there's a way my dad laughs that makes me think he has a lot more fun with Jeff than with me. I listen very carefully for that laugh when we cook or play games together. When it comes, it's almost the same as his Jeff laugh— but not quite.

Here's something else about my dad: He is much neater than my mom. He's always picking stuff up and folding clothes and grumbling about the mess. If we were a sitcom family, it would be my mom carrying on like that, talking about having to live with a house full of men! But my mom can be the biggest slob. Honestly. I mean, she's super nice, but she just doesn't care about things like dirty dishes or papers piling up on the dining-room table. Her motto is "Life is short and there will always be dirty dishes, so let's dance."

Did I mention my mother is funny, too? Her name is Penny. What's weird is that she has this copper-colored hair, which she swears no one knew she would have when they named her (she's the only one in her family with penny-colored hair). My dad says he fell in love with my mom because of her name and her hair, but I doubt he's that shallow. (I pride myself on being the truly shallow member of the family. Remember, *I* fell in love with feathery blond hair and a head shaped like a melon.)

My mom teaches second grade in a school a couple of towns away. I'll bet she's a really good teacher, even if she gets in trouble sometimes for having a messy room. (I hope she doesn't tell her kids her motto.) Half the time our kitchen table is piled up with her classroom projects. And she's always talking about her students like they're part of the family.

I never really thought about this before, but both my parents have jobs where they work with kids, and they're both always talking about how terrific "their" kids are— even my dad's "troubled teens," who he says only need love and direction—and, well, the part I never thought about before is this: Why do I keep worrying that they won't love me as much once they know "the truth" about me? They love everybody.

Aunt Pam says that a kid like me couldn't have better parents.

Oh, I have to tell you about Aunt Pam. She's my mom's younger sister— a lot younger. When I tell people that my aunt lives with us, they probably picture this old lady with her hair up in a bun who sits around all day chain-smoking and knitting baby booties for the starving children of Armenia.☺ But Aunt Pam is not like that at all. She is twenty-eight years old, and I think it is fair to say that if a vote were taken tomorrow, she would win the title of Most Beautiful Woman in All of Paintbrush Falls and Maybe Even All of Upstate New York. If Julia Roberts were her sister, Julia would be whining all the time, "Why can't *I* look like Pam? It's not fair!" I am *so* not kidding.

Aunt Pam is an artist. When she moved in with us a couple of years ago, my dad helped her turn the upstairs room over our garage into a studio. She makes these really big paintings that she says are abstract and all about feelings. I don't know about that. I know I like

---

☺ Mr. D: I don't really know if there are starving children in Armenia or how baby booties would help them. I don't even know if Armenia is a real place. Since this is a paper for English and not social studies, I won't lose points for making stuff up like this, will I? I am being creative. (Don't you think creativity should count for extra points?)

them, but maybe that's because I totally love Aunt Pam.

It's hard not to love somebody who is always on your side. When I was going through such a tough time in fifth grade, it was Aunt Pam who helped me know I'd be okay. I told her everything—even more than I told Bobby. And do you know what she would do? She'd sit there and nod her head and say, "That's cool." Like nothing I told her was a big deal! Then when I would finish, she would say, "You're good just the way you are, Joe. Life isn't always going to be easy—it isn't for anybody—but you've got the stuff and you're going to be so fine you'll shine." We'd laugh when she'd say that. It was so corny, that "so fine you'll shine" thing. But it really helped. It still does.

I guess I could believe anything Aunt Pam told me, because I knew she'd been through tough times herself. She moved in with us after living in New York City for a few years. It wasn't that she wanted to move to a small town, she just needed somebody to take care of her for a while and help her get back on her feet—"love and direction," as my dad says. She had a boyfriend in New York who wasn't good for her. I think there might have been drugs involved, and I hate to say it because it makes me so mad, but I'm pretty sure her boyfriend hit her sometimes and that's the main reason she had to get away. When she came to live with us, she looked a lot older than twenty-six, but the longer she stayed the younger she got.

Bobby has this major crush on Aunt Pam—or did until Kelsey came along and he got a girlfriend of his own. (And one his own age. Hello.) When he found out that Aunt Pam was going to move back to New York (which she's going to do after Christmas), he could hardly talk about it. I'm kind of glad he feels that way, because to be honest, I can hardly talk about it myself. I'm going to miss her soooo much. She says we'll IM and talk on the phone, but it won't be the same. She's my aunt, but in some ways she's my very best friend. She's the keeper of my secrets. She makes me feel so fine I shine.

She says I'll shine just as bright without her. We'll see.

I just reread everything I wrote about my family. I pretended I didn't know me or Jeff or my mom or dad or Aunt Pam, and I thought, *Wow, this is a pretty nice family.* Then I got thinking about Colin's family and how I'll bet he could write really nice things about them, too—but there's something, I don't know, different about them. I've been over to his house a few times now, and his mom and dad are very polite and try hard to make me feel welcome, and his little sister, whose name is Claire, is really cute (although weirdly well-behaved for a six-year-old), but I never feel entirely comfortable there. Everything *matches*. It's all so perfect—from the American flag flying out front to the cabinet in the family room full of trophies and awards (a lot of them Colin's). The magazines on the coffee table in the living room are fanned out like they belong in a doctor's office, and there isn't one picture on the walls that's even, like, a millimeter crooked.

Then there's Colin's room. It's nice and all, but it's not exactly what you'd expect a seventh-grade boy's room to look like. Neither is mine, of course, but it definitely looks like me. Colin's room looks like it belongs in one of the magazines on the coffee table downstairs. I asked him once if he'd picked out the furniture and pictures on the walls, and he just laughed and said, "As if." He told me his mom uses this decorator named Paul, who comes up from Albany and *he* makes all the decisions in their house. He said his mom thinks Paul is "brilliant," but his dad doesn't want to be there when Paul is around because "people like that" make him "uptight." When I asked Colin what his father meant by "people like that," Colin said, "You know," and changed the subject.

My other friends' families are nothing like Colin's.

They're more like mine, but funkier. Addie's family is the funkiest of the funky, even after her mom started shaving her armpits a few years ago (thank you, Lord). They all wear these really ugly sandals that should be totally banned—Birkensomethings—and the way they eat tofu 24/7 you'd think it actually tasted *good*, when in fact it has no taste at all! And they're always carrying on about the latest political outrage and the starving children of Armenia and animal rights and women's rights and Native American rights . . . and, well, their car has so many bumper stickers I swear it's a miracle they haven't caused, like, a zillion accidents. I mean, how are you supposed to read those things when you're zooming down the highway at a hundred miles an hour?☺

As for Skeezie, he lives with his mom and two younger sisters in this little ranch house (painted a truly unfortunate mushroom-soup color) over on Wellington. His dad left town a couple of years ago, and Skeezie hasn't seen him much since then. His mom works pretty hard, so Skeezie ends up having to take care of his two younger sisters a lot. I know he loves them and all, but I get the feeling he's not too happy having to act like a dad to

☺ Mr. D: Once again, I am being creative. Believe me, when I am old enough to drive, I will wear my seat belt and obey the speed limit. I do understand, however, that in Italy driving at a hundred miles per hour is *normale* (that's Italian for normal).

them sometimes. His house is even messier than mine, and everybody seems tired. His sisters—Megan and Jessie—are kind of whiny, but I think it's because they wish their mom was around more. When she's not working, Allison (that's their mom) tries to be a good parent, I think, but she has this habit of falling asleep. When that happens, Skeezie gets so angry at his dad for doing this to their family that he just grabs his sisters and takes them to the movies where they all pig out on popcorn and try to forget.

Bobby's family has had a hard time of it, too. His family is only him and his dad, Mike, because his mom died when he was seven. That's still kind of a hard thing for me to talk about because I loved his mom (she was a big hugger, like my dad), and I remember when she got sick, and it made me sad, but even more than that, it scared me to think that your mom could die. Bobby and his dad are really close, and Mike is nice to everybody and always orders out pizza for us when we hang out there— even though I know for a fact that they watch every dime they spend. Bobby even has to work part-time to help out.

The thing is, in all our families—mine and Addie's and Skeezie's and Bobby's—we have a lot of room to be whoever we are. (Aunt Pam said that to me once.) Even if

I haven't exactly told my parents everything about who I am, I guess I know deep down that it will be okay when I do, because they've never been uptight about, you know, the dolls and my dressing up and, until the lasagna incident, the Easy-Bake oven phase. Except for not wanting her to play with Barbies, Addie's parents have pretty much encouraged Addie to be her own true self. And Skeezie and Bobby—well, I think their parents are so busy worrying about putting food on the table that they can't be bothered with much more than making sure their kids don't get into trouble.

It's only Colin who doesn't have the room to be himself. He told me one time that his parents never get mad, they just get disappointed. I said, "You're lucky they don't get mad." He said, "I'd rather they *did* get mad." I think I said something brilliant back like, "Huh?" Because I didn't get it. But now I do. Totally.

LIFE LESSON FOR PARENTS: Love your kids. Let them play with Barbies. Let them pick out the stuff in their bedroom. (Hello.) And don't tell them that "people like that" make you uptight, because for all you know your kids just might be "people like that," too.

G is for
THE GANG OF FIVE

THE GANG OF FIVE IS WHAT BOBBY, SKEEZIE, ADDIE, AND I HAVE
CALLED OURSELVES SINCE THE SECOND GRADE. MISS HASKELL WAS
out of school for a week with the flu or something, and we
had this sub named Mrs. Esley, who, trust me, was a TOTAL
NIGHTMARE!☺ Anyway, Skeezie, trying to trick Mrs. Esley
into thinking he was a lot dumber than he is (which, no
offense to Skeezie, isn't that hard to do), kept giving her the
wrong answers to everything. For example, one day he
insisted that 2 + 2 = 5. At lunch he said, "We should call
ourselves the Gang of Five, because remember: Two plus
two equals five." This is an example of Skeezie's humor at
the time. He was *so* not funny.

Even though this happened in April, we didn't think
much about being the Gang of Five until the next fall.

☺ Mr. Daly: I'm sorry if Mrs. Esley is a personal friend of yours or your cousin or
something. I'm just being honest. Besides, she hasn't subbed in our school since
the second grade, so I'll bet I'm not the only one who thought she was bad news.

Remember how I said that Bobby's mom got real sick and died? Well, that happened during the summer after second grade. When we started school again in the fall, Bobby was quieter than ever (and if you know Bobby, you know he can be really quiet) (unlike *moi*). Even though he didn't come right out and say it, I think Skeezie and Addie and I understood that his being so quiet had to do with his being sad and maybe a little scared.

And then this really creepy thing happened.

We were out in the playground at recess, and this mean kid—I don't remember his name because he had just moved here and he moved away a month later, so I'll just call him MK (for "mean kid")—came over and said to Bobby, "What's your name?"

Bobby said, "Bobby."

MK said, "That's not your name."

Bobby: It is, too.

MK: It is not. I heard it's Little *Orphan* Bobby.

Bobby: What is that supposed to mean?

MK: It means your *mommy* died. So you're an *orphan*!

Then he started singing this "Little Orphan Bobby" song he made up! Bobby's eyes got all, like, watery. Skeezie told MK he was a jerk. I told him he was a *double* jerk. And when he wouldn't shut up, Addie slugged him.

MK said he was going to tell the principal, but Addie

said if he did, *she* would tell the principal what he'd said to Bobby, and Mrs. Wishnie would punish him by making him clean every single toilet in the whole school. For the rest of his life. With his bare hands.

(I never thought about it before, but maybe that's why he moved away.)

Anyway, afterwards Bobby said thanks to everybody for sticking up for him, and Skeezie said, "No sweat. We're the Gang of Five, remember?" And that's when we remembered we *were* the Gang of Five, and we've never forgotten.

It's more than just being friends, this Gang of Five thing. We need each other. We're the kids the other kids make fun of. (Although maybe that's changing now that three out of four of us are going out with kids who are more or less popular.) The problem is that the kids who have laughed at us or called us names have never bothered to get to know us. All they see is this fat and quiet kid (Bobby). And this tall, skinny, and *not* quiet girl. (Earth to Addie: It's okay to shut up once in a while!) And . . . well, I'm not sure what they see when they look at Skeezie. He's got this whole 1950s, Elvis Presley kind of thing going, and, as more than one teacher has been known to remark, he "marches to his own drummer." I guess you could say that's true of me, too, but with me, it would be more like, "He dances to his own soundtrack."

Anyway, we have each other and we don't really care

what other people say about us. We know that the Gang of Five totally rocks. And now, after running for student council a few weeks ago (and losing, but, oh, well) and actually having the nerve to get up in front of the entire school at the campaign assembly, maybe we're not the only ones who think so.☺

Starting at the beginning of the sixth grade, we (the Gang of Five) have met every week for something called the Forum (Addie came up with the name) (I still don't get it), which is where we meet at the Candy Kitchen and talk about Important, News-Breaking, World-Shaking Topics while eating ice cream or other junky food. Addie usually comes up with the Important, News-Breaking, World-Shaking Topics (which are so *not*), and she writes down everything we say. Personally, I don't think everything we say deserves to be written down, but it's easier just to let Addie have her way about most stuff so she can think she's the genius of the century.

☺ Mr. D: I know you know all of this, but you told us to assume that the reader knows nothing. So here's the background on the election: Addie came up with the not-very-brilliant idea of creating a third political party to run for student council. She called it the Freedom Party. Then Bobby *made* it brilliant by changing it to the No-Name Party and saying, "If elected, we will work to end name-calling here at Paintbrush Falls Middle School." Well, the Democrats won (we came in a close second), and that was okay, really, because for once the Republicans and Brittney "Ha, Ha, I'm Popular and You're Not!" Hobson didn't win an election, and the second reason it was okay was that Colin won as vice president. But the point is, Bobby gave this great speech that was right out of a movie, with people cheering and everything. And Mr. Kiley was so impressed with Bobby's idea of having a No-Name Day that he promised he would help us make it happen.

These are the minutes from our last Forum:

Addie: Today's topic is "What I'd Do for Love."

Skeezie: Do we barf now or after we've eaten?

Joe: That is so CosmoGIRL!

Addie: Meaning?

Joe: Meaning: cool!

Skeezie: Well, I don't think it's cool. Just because the three of you have gone and fallen all goo-goo in love doesn't mean I have to roll around in it.

Bobby: Roll around in what?

Skeezie: The goo-goo. The mess. What are you looking at?

Joe: The goo-goo? You are so strange.

Skeezie: "Thank you. Thank you very much."☺ But can we please talk about something else?

Addie: Like what?

Skeezie: Like when is our food going to get here?

Addie: All you think about is food.

Skeezie: Why shouldn't I? You can eat food. You can't eat love.

Joe: Ooo. Addie, did you write that down? "You can't eat love." Brilliant. Can't you just picture it on a T-shirt?

Skeezie: Shut up, doofus.

☺ Skeezie trying to sound like Elvis Presley.

Joe: Be nice, Schuyler.☺ No name-calling, remember?

Addie: Thank you, Joe. What I wanted to say was this: Yesterday, DuShawn said this kind of mean thing about somebody—

Joe: Who?

Addie: It doesn't matter. Anyway, I'm embarrassed to admit this, but . . . well, when he said it, I just kind of let it go.

Bobby: What do you mean?

Addie: I didn't <u>say</u> anything.

Skeezie: Wait. Addie Carle, whose first words were "In <u>my</u> opinion," didn't say anything?

Addie: That's right. And then I thought, Oh, no, I'm letting him get away with this because . . . because, you know . . .

Skeezie: Because you loooooooove him.

Addie: Shut <u>up</u>. But yes.

Bobby: Maybe you didn't want to make him feel bad by pointing out that he was being stupid.

Addie: He wasn't just being stupid, he was being mean.

Joe: What did he say?

Addie: It doesn't matter.

Joe: Was it about me?

☺ Skeezie's real name.

Addie: No, Joe. It was not about you or any of us. It was about someone in his family, if you must know, and I don't want to repeat what he said. The point is, if you love somebody—and Skeezie, if you start singing some dumb Elvis song,☺ I'll squeeze this entire ketchup bottle down your shirt, I swear—if you love somebody, do you go along with them even when you don't feel right about it?

Joe: Hmm. I know what you mean. Colin wants to keep our going out a secret—and I understand, I really do, but at the same time . . .

Addie: At the same time, that is so last century.

Joe: Right. But I don't want him to feel bad or break up with me, so I'm going along with it.

Addie: What about you and Kelsey, Bobby?

Bobby: Oh, we don't have any problems. Of course, we don't talk much.

Skeezie: Big surprise there.

Addie: I don't know. Sometimes I think it's easier to stand up to the whole school—or the whole world even—than it is to stand up to one person, especially if that person really matters to you.

☺ Ever since Steffi, the waitress at the Candy Kitchen who Skeezie has a crush on (even though he won't admit it), started calling him Elvis, Skeezie has memorized all these old Elvis songs. He even imitates Elvis when he sings them. You might think this would be funny or even cool. Trust me, you'd be so wrong.

Bobby:	That makes sense to me. I have trouble telling my dad things sometimes. I don't want to let him down.
Joe:	It's the same with me and my dad.
Addie:	But you both have the best dads.
Bobby:	So do you.
Skeezie:	Okay, another thing? Can we not talk about who has the best dad? Oh, hey, our food! Oh, man, I didn't ask for a BLT! I asked for a grilled cheese with bacon!

At that point, Addie stopped taking notes. It almost always ends up like this. We talk until the food shows up. Then, no matter what Skeezie has ordered, there's something wrong with it, and he has to throw a hissy fit and be a big drama queen about it. We never get back to what we were talking about. But that's okay because there's always the next time—and, trust me, Addie *never* runs out of Important, News-Breaking, World-Shaking Topics to talk about.

LIFE LESSON: As somebody said in a song once (I don't think it was Elvis), "You gotta have friends."

H is for
HALLOWEEN OKAY, SO HALLOWEEN IS MY ABSOLUTE,

numero uno favorite holiday. I mean, come on, we're talking about DRESSING UP here! Ever since I can remember, I have loved dressing up. And I'm not just talking about in my mother's clothes. Although: Been there, done that. There's this video of me when I was about three parading around the house in my mom's *very* high heels (I was also wearing one of her necklaces, my Oscar the Grouch underpants, a tutu, and a Superman cape). Anyway, every time we show this video it's a real crowd-pleaser—up until the part where *I fall down the stairs and MY FATHER KEEPS TAPING!* Everybody goes, like, "Dave, how could you have done that?!" I don't know, maybe he thought he'd win a million dollars on *America's Funniest Home Videos* or something, but this was his child's *life* we're talking about! Fine. It was only, like, two steps and there was knee-deep carpeting everywhere, but still.

Anyway, the point is that I *love* to dress up, and not only on Halloween. It's just that Halloween makes it legit. Even my brother dressed up in drag one Halloween a couple of years ago, although he was all very "Yuck, yuck, look at me, I'm a woman, watch me jiggle my melons and shake my booty." So gross. Not to mention Guy-Guy Behavior Supreme-O. In fact, they weren't melons, they were soccer balls. He must have used up a whole roll of duct tape to keep them on. My mother told him there was no way he was leaving the house looking like a walking silicone nightmare, and he said if I could dress up in girls' clothes why couldn't he, and Mom said that *I* wasn't insulting women when I did it. That's when he stormed out of the house, shouting, "Double standard!" Which surprised me, because I didn't think he even knew what "double standard" meant.

(This may have been around the time Addie came to her senses, in terms of my brother not being suitable crush material.)

It's funny. Even though I have done lots of dressing up in girls' clothes around the house, I have never worn drag on Halloween. Okay, almost never. I *was* Dorothy in kindergarten. But being Dorothy from *The Wizard of Oz* is kind of like being Mary in the Christmas pageant. Sacred-like, you know?

Anyway, I am *so* looking forward to Halloween this year. A whole group of us is going trick-or-treating (we figure it's our Farewell Tour, since we're kind of outgrowing it), and then we're going back to Addie's house for a party. I hope we get lots of candy, because I can just imagine what the refreshments will be like. This is a family that every Thanksgiving has *tofurky*.☺

Colin and I have been talking about our costumes for the last two weeks. We want to do something where we kind of go together—like salt and pepper, or Rose and Jack. (*Titanic.*) (Hello.) We actually considered that last one, thinking we could go as the part where they're floating around in the icy water. We were going to, like, cover ourselves in blue makeup and make little icicles to hang off our noses, but then we figured if my mother wouldn't let Jeff out of the house with his Pamela Anderson boobs, she was not about to let us go anywhere dressed as half-dead disaster victims. Besides which, we had already come to the conclusion all on our own that the idea would be Breaking New Ground in Bad Taste. (Although maybe Aunt Pam already did that with the *Titanic* cake.)

☺ Tofu shaped like a turkey. I am so not kidding.

Oh, and dressing up as *lovers*? And one of us being a *woman*? And going out in *public*? Uh. No.

It was Pam who came up with the brilliant idea of Bert and Ernie.

Okay, I have to admit this right here, right now. I totally love Bert and Ernie. Personally, I think it's not only un-American not to love Bert and Ernie, but *so* uncool.

Problem was, both Colin and I wanted to be Bert. But since Colin is taller, he won. I don't mind. I do Ernie's laugh better, anyway. And, needless to say, I have in my possession a rubber ducky. More than one. Okay, five.

So Pam is making our costumes and doing our hair and makeup and everything. No plastic masks for us! "Right, Bert?" "Right, Ernie!"☺

I'm going to write more later. Bye for now! And . . .

Happy Halloween!

It is now later.

How do I put this? Let's try: THIS WAS THE WORST HALLOWEEN OF MY LIFE!! And on top of that: I may have lost my one true love (i.e., Bert) forever!!

I am *so* not being dramatic.

☺ You'll have to imagine their voices, but believe me, when Colin and I do them, we sound so real, it's, like, "Hello, send our mail to Sesame Street!"

Okay, where do I start?

Our costumes were Fab. U. Luss. Except for our heads, which remained melon-instead-of-football-shaped, we looked *just* like Bert and Ernie. Besides being a painter, Pam works in the cosmetics department at Awkworth & Ames Department Store, so she was able to put together this perfect yellow and orange makeup (yellow for Bert/Colin, orange for Ernie/me). She put it on our faces and over these bald caps she found somewhere and added long strands of black crepe hair (the kind you make fake beards out of) to the tops of our heads. And she made a unibrow out of the same stuff for Colin that looked just like the one Bert has. By the time we put on the big noses and the costumes she'd made (I don't know how she found material that looked just like their shirts, but she did) (she's awesome) (she could be a Hollywood designer, I mean it), we could have been celebrity doubles!

Everybody was like, "Oh. My. God. You guys are *amazing!*"

And nobody had to guess who or what we were, unlike Addie, who was a stalk of broccoli, but most people thought she was either an alien or the Jolly Green Giant.

Anyway, trick-or-treating: Let's see, it was Colin and me; Bobby and Kelsey; Kelsey's friends Amy and Evie; Skeezie and his sisters, Megan and Jessie; Addie; Drew and

Sara (Sara broke up with Justin last week and is now Drew's girlfriend) (we think) (nobody's really sure about that); and Colin's sister, Claire. DuShawn didn't come with us because he said trick-or-treating was for little kids and he'd meet us at Addie's for the party later. If he had come with us in the first place, he might still have said what he did, but it wouldn't have been nearly as bad.

Anyway, up until the bad part we were having a really good time. Colin and I kept going, "Hey, Bert!" and "What is it, Ernie?" and cracking everybody up with our voices, and it was decided that we had to be the ones to say "trick or treat" at every house because the sound of it made people laugh even before they opened their doors—and then when they did open their doors, well, they freaked when they saw us, what can I say?

For almost an hour, it was the best Halloween ever. Colin and I walked together the whole time, being Bert and Ernie and sometimes holding Claire's hands between us and swinging her up in the air. She was dressed as the flying carpet from *Aladdin* (a hand-me-down, store-bought costume, but on her totally cute), so of course she had to fly. It was so much fun being the three of us. It was like, I don't know, Colin and I were *connected* through Claire or something. Almost like we were holding each other's hands instead of hers.

Anyway, we came to this street corner and everybody started to run across. Colin went to grab Claire's hand, but she had already gone ahead with Bobby and Kelsey, so he grabbed mine instead. By mistake, like. I guess I should have gone, "Bert, let go of my hand!" But I didn't. And he didn't let go. We ran across the street together like that—you know, holding hands. For all of maybe five seconds.

Guess who was watching from the other side.

DuShawn and Kevin and Jimmy.

DuShawn looks at us and goes, "Bert and Ernie? That is so gay."

If that had been all, it would have been okay. I mean, not okay, but we could have told him he was being a jerk and it would have been over. But Kevin had seen us holding hands, I guess, because he said, "That's because they *are* gay."

DuShawn said, "Huh?"

Kevin goes, "Bert and Ernie. They're gay. I mean, you never see them with girls, do you? They live together, right? Next thing you know, they'll be getting *married*. Hey, maybe that's what Colin and Joseph*ine* are gonna do."

"That is so sick," Jimmy Lemon says, and he and Kevin start making barf noises.

At that point, I don't remember who said what. I

probably should have told Kevin and Jimmy to shove it, but I heard somebody else saying it for me, and, besides, I was too busy watching the look of panic spreading over Colin's face under his yellow makeup. Addie was yelling at DuShawn, and DuShawn was yelling at Addie and then telling her he was sorry and then telling Kevin and Jimmy the two of them had better go. Which they did, but not before Kevin said something about faggots holding hands. I guess the whole thing didn't last more than a minute or two, but it seemed a lot longer.

On the way to Addie's house, Claire asked Colin if Bert and Ernie really were gay, and Colin said, "Of course not. Anyway, does it matter?" Claire thought about it and said, "Not really." "So don't worry about it," Colin told her. But from the way he avoided looking at me, I had the feeling he wasn't exactly taking his own advice.

At one point, I heard DuShawn say to Addie, "They were asking for it, dressing up like Bert and Ernie. I mean, what do they want people to think?"

"Are you blaming the *victims*?" Addie said, and then she was yelling again, and DuShawn was going, "I'm not saying that, I'm not saying that," until finally he agreed that maybe he *was* saying that, and for, like, the thousandth time he was sorry.

The party was over before it began—and not because of the food, which was actually pretty good. (Addie's parents are fantastic cooks, even if all their cookbooks have lame names like *The Joy of Soy*.) It's just that we were all feeling weird, especially since a few of the kids there knew about Colin and me, but most didn't, and now those who didn't were probably wondering.

Colin was still avoiding me. I tried getting him to talk by being Ernie, but that just got him annoyed (I could tell by his furrowed unibrow), and finally he said it was getting late and he should take Claire home.

Late? It was, like, eight o'clock—on a Friday night!

I went home pretty soon after that myself. Like I said, the party was *so* over. Before I changed out of my costume, I went online and e-mailed Colin.

Subject: Ernie to Bert
Date: October 31
From: phonehome217
To: blackbirdboy

Hi Bert,
That was fun tonight. Except for when Dumb, Dumber, and Dumberer showed up. Did Claire have fun? She sure is cute.

So write me, okay? Me and R.D. (Rubber Ducky) are lonely. What? What did you say, Bert? I can't hear you. I've got a banana in my ear.

Ernie

I checked my e-mail three times before I finally went to bed. I didn't hear from Colin, but Addie wrote to ask, RUOK? I sent back the shortest e-mail I ever wrote in my whole life: No. I mean, what else was there to say?

LIFE LESSON: Trick-or-treating is for little kids.

NOVEMBER

I is for
INSTANT MESSAGE

Subject: RUOK?

Date: November 2

From: phonehome217

To: blackbirdboy

Hi Colin,

Are you mad at me? You haven't e-mailed all weekend and when I tried calling you, Claire said you'd call back but you didn't. Maybe she didn't tell you I called? I'm sorry about Halloween but it isn't my fault some people are jerks. Are you sorry we dressed up as B&E? I'm not. I thought we were way cool and so did

blackbirdboy: hi ernie

phonehome217: hey bert! I was just writing you! I mean, Joe was just writing Colin. ruok?

blackbirdboy: yeah. sorry I didn't call you back. How was the rest of the party?

phonehome217: you mean the party that wasn't?

blackbirdboy: yeah, that one. Drew says it sucked.

phonehome217: Drew is right.

blackbirdboy: Sara broke up with Drew and went back to Justin. Drew is all mopey. Sara told Justin about Halloween.

phonehome217: what about it?

blackbirdboy: going trick-or-treating, the party, everybody's costumes. Justin told her it sounded lame

phonehome217: How do you know what Justin said?

blackbirdboy: Justin told Drew & drew told me

phonehome217: oh / Justin and drew are speaking to each other?

blackbirdboy: yeah, they're good friends

phonehome217: weird

blackbirdboy: when I got home on friday you know what my dad said? He said, what are you supposed to be? I told him Bert. He said, from Sesame Street? That's kind of gay, isn't it? My own DAD said it!

phonehome217: why would he say that? He's supposed to be a grown-up!

blackbirdboy: meaning?

phonehome217: meaning grown-ups aren't supposed to call things gay

blackbirdboy: I think my dad's got a hang-up about it.

phonehome217: Why?

blackbirdboy: He always says these things. Like what he said about Paul the decorator, remember?

phonehome217: yeah. so what did you say back?

blackbirdboy: nothing. it made me feel sick, really sick, like I was going to throw up

phonehome217: DID YOU?

blackbirdboy: no, but I ran upstairs and got out of that costume real fast

phonehome217: is that why you're not speaking 2 me?

blackbirdboy: I'm not not speaking to you / I just needed to think about stuff

phonehome217: RU about to break up with me? Because if you are you should do it in person or at least on the phone!!!!!!!!!

blackbirdboy: I AM NOT BREAKING UP WITH YOU!!!!!!

phonehome217: but you wouldn't talk to me at the party and you didn't call me back

blackbirdboy: can I tell you something? will you shut up and not interrupt me and be all worried I'm going to break up with you?

phonehome217: moi? shut up?

blackbirdboy: I'm waiting

phonehome217: ok ok

blackbirdboy: ok . . . so . . . here's what I think / you've had lots of time to know what it's like being gay. Because you were always different and maybe it was just obvious to you that's what you were. I just figured it out last year and at first I was all like no this can't be me, I can't be this way! but then I

blackbirdboy: saw a couple of gay characters on tv and I thought how they could be me and then I read this book with these three teenage guys figuring out they were gay and one of them was so much like me I couldn't believe it and then there were these signals. Like, I love playing sports but part of it is that I like being

blackbirdboy: with other guys so much and then there were these other feelings

phonehome217: I know what you mean

blackbirdboy: yeah well it kind of scared me to have those feelings, but then I guessed that even though we were different in lots of ways maybe you had the same kinds of feelings and the more I watched you the more I thought you were pretty cool and I wished I could be like you AND DON'T INTERRUPT ME. the thing is that even if

blackbirdboy: I can handle what it feels like to be gay inside I don't know if I can handle what other people do with it. I think maybe it was a mistake to have dressed up like we did and it was a BOG mistake to hold hands like that. It was stupid

phonehome217: thanx a lot / and what do you mean a BOG mistake?

blackbirdboy: sorry / a BIG mistake / and you know what I mean and I don't mean I think we're stupid or you're stupid / I mean it was stupid to hold hands like that

phonehome217: "I want to hold your hand." The Beatles

blackbirdboy: "Take these broken wings and learn to fly." The Beatles

phonehome217: what's that from

blackbirdboy: "Blackbird"

phonehome217: so that's why you're blackbirdboy

blackbirdboy: yeah, it's my fave beatles song and you're phonehome because of E.T.—but why 217?

phonehome217: birthday—feb 17

blackbirdboy: I knew that

phonehome217: you did?

blackbirdboy: sure. Last year—remember?

phonehome217: yeah, you said a little bird told you. who was . . . ?

blackbirdboy: "blackbird singing in the dead of night"

phonehome217: ?????

blackbirdboy: I'm the bird who told me. I saw it on a paper in the school office one time

phonehome217: when you wished me happy birthday I couldn't believe it. You were my birthday wish

blackbirdboy: wow! really?

phonehome217: no, I'm lying. YES REALLY! So when is your bday?

blackbirdboy: aug. 2

phonehome217: You're a LEO?!?!?!?!

blackbirdboy: why is that surprising?

phonehome217: you don't seem like a leo. I should be a Leo and you should be me—Aquarius

blackbirdboy: do you believe in that stuff?

phonehome217: not really

blackbirdboy: what do you want for your birthday?

phonehome217: "I want to hold your hand." The Beatles

blackbirdboy: "I am only waiting for the moment to be free." The Beatles

phonehome217: huh?

blackbirdboy: i'm not ready to hold hands—in public and stuff. I'm sorry, 'cause I know you want to be more "out of the closet" and all that

phonehome217: it's okay

blackbirdboy: really?

phonehome217: yeah, I'll just have to wait until your moment to be free. hey, isn't it weird that we both know so much about the Beatles and E.T. and Bert and Ernie? Are we like retro or something

blackbirdboy: I guess

phonehome217: so how about those Yankees huh?

blackbirdboy: WHAT?

phonehome217: I ran out of things to say. Do you wish I liked sports?

blackbirdboy: no. do you wish I wanted to get my ear pierced like you do?

phonehome217: DO YOU WANT TO? Next weekend, we could do it!

blackbirdboy: Repeat: DO YOU WISH I WANTED TO GET MY EAR PIERCED (WHICH I DO NOT)?

phonehome217: I kind of do, but it's ok

blackbirdboy: my dad's yelling at me to get off the computer. I'll see you in school tomorrow ok?

phonehome217: ok

blackbirdboy: so like sweet dreams and stuff ok?

phonehome217: U2

blackbirdboy: hey ernie

phonehome217: what is it bert

blackbirdboy: Ernie, you've got a banana in your ear

phonehome217: I'm sorry, Bert. I can't hear you. I've got a banana in my ear.

blackbirdboy: LOL

phonehome217: LOL TTFN

blackbirdboy: TTFN

LIFE LESSON (OR QUESTION): There's a song (not the Beatles) that says we're "born free," so how come we have to wait?

J is for
JOE
OKAY, I'M SURE J COULD BE FOR OTHER THINGS,
BUT THIS IS *MY* ALPHABIOGRAPHY, SO J *HAS* TO BE
for Joe. The only problem is, I don't know what to write.
I just finished IM-ing with Colin, and that's all I can
think about.

Well, maybe not all. I'm thinking about tomorrow, too.
Monday. Back to school. Wondering if Kevin and Jimmy
will say anything about seeing Colin and me holding
hands.

Oh. My. God. What if they *do*?

I may have to call in dead.☺

Soooo . . . to get my mind off Colin (♥) and Kevin and
Jimmy (☹) . . . I'm going to go interview my parents about
when I was a baby and stuff. Maybe that will help me
figure out what to write.

☺ Joke. Bad taste. Sorry.

J is for Joe: The Early Years

I, Joseph Daniel Bunch, was born twelve years and almost nine months ago in a hospital in Albany, New York. My mother says I looked straight into her eyes when we met, so she knew right off I was going to be special. (She just didn't know *how* special, right?) My dad says the first time he saw me I was so skinny he called me "String Bean." Those were his first words to me: string bean. Nice.

My first word was "poo." I know what you're thinking, but you are so wrong. It was because I had a Winnie-the-Pooh doll that I took everywhere with me. I still have him. He's my favorite of all my stuffed animals. And, yes, I still have all my stuffed animals and I don't care who knows it! (Except maybe Kevin and Jimmy.)

According to my mom, I showed an early "creative flair," meaning that I liked dressing up and playing make-believe from when I was very little. She said she couldn't keep me out of her closet, so she finally gave me some of her old clothes and made a dress-up trunk out of a box this big truck from my grandparents had come in. (Hated the truck, loved the box.) I called the box my "mannabah." To this day, nobody knows what I meant by that, and I am sure I have no idea.

One thing I remember from the early years is my uncle Scott's wedding, which happened soon after we moved to Paintbrush Falls. Uncle Scott is my dad's younger brother. He likes to say he makes his money making money. I used to think that meant he was in his basement printing up counterfeit bills. Then I realized he didn't have a basement. My dad says his job has something to do with banking. Whatever. Frankly, Uncle Scott is kind of a snob, but I didn't know that back then. All I knew was that I got to dress up in my best clothes— I actually liked wearing ties, what can I tell you?—and go to this grown-up party in Schenectady.

The wedding was awesome, especially at the beginning when Aunt Lainy walked down the aisle and at the end when she and Uncle Scott kissed. Uncle Scott is very handsome and Aunt Lainy is very beautiful, so it was sort of like a fairy tale. Besides, I liked kissing. I called it "getting smoochy."

The party afterwards was even more awesome than the wedding. There was this huge bowl of fizzy punch with different colors of sherbet floating around in it and a *fountain* in the middle of it! And the wedding cake, which must have been taller than I was, had, like, a zillion sugar flowers all over it, with little gold leaves! Looking back, I'll bet the whole thing was way tacky, but at the time I felt like I was in a *movie*.

That was the beginning of my wedding obsession. I had this doll Aunt Pam gave me (she had me so figured out) (a lot more than my poor grandparents, who gave me a fire engine for Christmas the year after the truck) (again: loved the box).

Anyway, I wanted a wedding dress for the doll— formerly known as Cinderella Beauty and renamed Lainy—and Mom took me to the mall, but we couldn't find one, so she got this woman she knew to make one that would look just like Aunt Lainy's dress. It took more than a month, and when we finally went to pick it up, I practically peed in my pants I was so excited. But when the woman saw me, she laughed and said, "I never made a doll's dress for a *boy* before!" I totally wanted to die.

(This was my first clue that maybe to other people there was something "wrong" with me.) (Not that it stopped me from dressing up or playing wedding.)

My mom says that I played wedding for about a year and that I kept asking everybody if they would marry me. Even Jeff. (That was the only time anyone can remember Jeff threatening to clobber me on a regular basis.) I had my Lainy doll marry my Ken doll. I also had her marry some of my

Barbies. And G.I. Joe. (I hated that the soldier doll had my name. I mean, please. I didn't play with him much. He was another Christmas present from my clueless grandparents. One time when they were visiting, my grandpa asked me if G.I. Joe had been in any wars lately. I said, "No, but he and Ken got married last week." Every Christmas since then, my grandparents have sent me a check.)

J is for Joe: The Middle Years

I'm in the middle years now. I mean, not really, but I'm counting my future as the "later years." So this is me now:

1. I am 5' 2" tall.
2. I weigh 98 pounds. (Kind of skinny, but not a string bean.)
3. I have thick, wavy, medium-brown hair, currently streaked with red.
4. I have dark brown, close-set eyes. (On some people close-set eyes can be attractive. I'll have to wait and see what the rest of my face does.)
5. My nose is too big. (Not much hope there.) (Curse you, paternal genes!)
6. I have nice ears. Not that ears matter much, but at least they don't stick out like Jeff's. His

friends used to call him Dumbo. (Note to parents, if I ever let them read this: I have *perfect* ears for an earring.)

7. I *love* clothes! Right now, I'm into oversize, long-sleeved shirts (oxford button-downs, mostly), which I wear over colored T-shirts. In warmer weather, I like wearing these big, baggy Hawaiian shirts (also over colored T-shirts). I'm into cargo pants or baggy jeans or shorts, worn with oversize belts. Or sometimes I wear these totally retro dress pants I find at the thrift shop on Main Street. What can I say? I have a *fabulous* and totally original sense of style.

Now that I think of it, Colin has never said he likes the way I dress. He's also never said anything about liking my streaked hair or the way I paint the pinky fingernail on my right hand. (Actually, Aunt Pam paints it for me. She does all these amazing tiny pictures. Like, right now, I have a sun/moon face.)

Oh. My. God. Maybe Colin hates my clothes and my hair and my fingernail. Maybe he wishes

I wore the kind of boring shirts he wears, with their Easter colors and little polo guys on them. Colin is pretty Ralph Lauren, when you come right down to it. So is his whole family. I'm sorry, I would rather eat raw tofurky than wear cotton pullovers with little thingies on them—polo guys, sailboats, whatever that Tommy Hilfiger logo is supposed to be. I am *so* not into logos.

What if Colin and I are incompatible?!?!?!?☺ What if I get an earring and he goes, "Ewww"?

This is *so* Romeo and Juliet! True love torn apart by tragic differences!

8. I just reread what I wrote, and I thought, *I sound so shallow!* That's what Addie would say, anyway. She's all about thinking about things, and I'm all about how things look. Well, excuse me, but it's not like I never think. And one thing I *think* is that appearances matter. It tells the rest of the world who you are. And who I am is Totally, Awesomely Stylin', Thank You Very Much.

9. So, okay, some other things about me:

a. I love cats, but my mom's allergic, so we can't have any. When I need my feline

---

☺ Mr. D: I'm pretty sure this is the right word. I looked it up.

fix, I go next door and hang with Addie's cats, Kennedy and Johnson.

b. English is my favorite subject!!!!!!!!☺

c. I hate Phys Ed. (Duh.)

d. I love brownies and ice cream. (Especially peppermint stick ice cream. The Candy Kitchen makes this only at Christmas, which is totally unfair.)

e. Christmas is my second-favorite holiday. My family gets into it big time. (Even if my mother is one-quarter Jewish.) (Which I guess makes me one-eighth Jewish.) (Who says I can't do fractions?)

f. I like movies, music, and magazines.

g. I also like books, but I wish there were more books about boys like me. I mean, most of the books "for boys" are about guy-guys. The characters are always trapped in the wilderness, where they become friends with a wolf, or their biggest worry in life is how they're going to score the winning point for the team. Yawn.

h. I love to daydream, especially about the future.

☺ Mr. D: I am *so* not making this up!

J is for Joe: The Later Years

So, what is my future? Well, I'll probably live in a big city—New York or Paris or Hollywood. I mean, I so don't see myself in Paintbrush Falls for the rest of my life! And I'll probably be famous. I don't know at what, but I've got time to figure that out. I was thinking about being an actor or a singer, but I'd *hate* having to deal with the paparazzi all the time! And the *fans*! Always bugging you for your autograph. And some of them are totally crazy and live in the bushes outside your house, and then you have to have bodyguards. (Having bodyguards might be fun, but I don't want people living in my bushes. That is *so* creepy!)

With my natural style sense and all, maybe I'll be a fashion designer. If I am, I will *not* use logos!!!!!!

The only other thing I think about the future is that I definitely want to get married and have kids. What I forgot to say before is that during my wedding obsession year I insisted that my mother buy all the bridal magazines at the supermarket checkout. She was, like, "But honey, you don't know how to read yet." Hello, who *reads* bridal magazines? Of course, when I get married there isn't going to be a bride, although it might be fun to ask Jeff to strap on some soccer balls and be my maid of honor.

I wonder if Colin wants to get married someday, too.

(I just remembered what Kevin and Jimmy said about Bert and Ernie getting married and about that being so sick it made them want to puke and all.) (They're the ones who are sick.) (Kevin and Jimmy, I mean.) (Totally.)

LIFE LESSON: There should be a magazine called *Grooms*.

K is NOT for
KISSING

OH. MY. GOD. YOU ARE SO NOT GOING TO BELIEVE WHAT HAPPENED on Monday! Okay, remember how in J I said I was worried that Kevin and Jimmy were going to tell everybody they saw Colin and me holding hands? Well, guess what. It was a whole lot worse! By the end of third period it was all over school that Colin and I had been seen kissing!

I mean, hello. *Kissing?!*

Third period happened to be art, which is one of three classes Colin and I have together. We were coming from English (which we also have together) when we heard all this giggling and laughing and "They did *not!*" and "They did *so!*" coming from the art room. The minute they saw us, everybody went, "Shh, shh, shh," and turned their heads away, acting like we weren't there. Some of the girls were still giggling, though, and some of the boys were making kissy noises and punching each other on the shoulder. Kevin and Jimmy aren't even in our art class, but I was, like, one thousand percent sure they were behind whatever was going on.

I looked across the room at Bobby, who rolled his eyes and shook his head, which didn't tell me anything. I was all set to go over and ask him what was up, when Mr. Minelli came in and told everybody to get to their tables and take out their sketchbooks.

Ordinarily, I am very happy that Colin and I sit next to each other in art. Mr. Minelli lets the class talk in low voices while we work, and Colin and I have this goofy thing we do where he's Moonet, the famous cow artist, and I'm Pigasso, who draws three-eyed pigs playing guitars. We have other goofy routines, too, and we're always making each other laugh and then bumping elbows to make each other stop. Sometimes, I think we do it just as an excuse to bump elbows. But no way were we bumping elbows on Monday. We weren't even talking to each other!

When the bell rang, Colin grabbed his backpack, mumbled something about having to meet up with Drew, and was out the door before I was even out of my seat. I turned to Kelsey, who sits on the other side of me, and said, "Okay, what is going on?"

Her hair was hanging over her face, so I wasn't sure I heard right at first, but when I asked her a second time, I got it: "Everybody says you and Colin were kissing."

"*What?* That's ridiculous!"

I expected her to say, "I know," but instead she said, "Well, what if you were? It's nobody's business."

Bobby came around from the other side of the table then, and the three of us kept talking while we walked to history. It turned out that seeing us holding hands wasn't good enough for Kevin and Jimmy (a.k.a. The Twin Faces of Evil). No, they had to tell the whole school they'd seen us *kissing.* When I reminded Bobby and Kelsey that they'd been with Colin and me the whole time, so they knew it wasn't true, Bobby said that Kevin said it happened when we were standing by ourselves waiting to cross the street and no one was looking.

"Look, Joe," he said. "I don't care if you and Colin kissed. It's not a big deal, okay? It's just so unfair that Kevin and Jimmy—"

"The Twin Faces of Evil," I corrected him.

"Fine. The Twin Faces of Evil. It's just unfair of them to spread it around school."

"*But we weren't kissing!*"

Bobby nodded, like, *uh-huh, whatever.*

I know I said before that I liked kissing, that I called it "getting smoochy" and all that. But that was when I was little and wasn't talking about doing the kissing myself. Not *that* kind of kissing, anyway. I mean, bumping elbows is one thing, and holding hands is awesome, but actually putting your mouth on somebody else's mouth and exchanging saliva?☺ *Ewww!*

It got even worse after history. We went to our lockers. Mine had I ♥ COLIN on it, and Colin's, which is across the hall from mine, had I ♥ JOE on it. Kelsey said we should report it to Mr. Kiley right away, but I said no, because I didn't know if Colin had even seen it and I didn't want to make things worse for him. Luckily, we were able to get the writing off both lockers pretty easily with some paper towels and soap. (Whoever did it must have used really cheap markers.) (As if I don't know who did it.) While we were waiting for Colin to show up so we could walk to lunch together, I made Bobby and Kelsey promise they wouldn't tell him what had happened.

But Colin never showed up, so we walked to the cafeteria by ourselves. Guess where he was! Not at our table, where he'd been sitting for weeks. No, he and Drew were at their old table, sitting with their other friends. I couldn't believe this was happening. It was even worse

☺ Mr. D: Sorry to have to get all R-rated.

than the Halloween party. It was like he'd turned me invisible—and all because of a stupid rumor that wasn't true! I started to go over to his table, but Bobby pulled me back.

"Don't, Joe," he said. "Just leave him alone."

I knew he was right. Whatever I would have said or done would only have made it worse.

It was then that I noticed how everybody was whispering and looking back and forth between me and Colin. Well, maybe not everybody, but it totally felt that way.

When we got to our table, Addie was blabbing away about what an outrage this kissing thing was, and how we needed to do something about it, and what we needed to do was start a GSA.

"A what?" I said.

"A GSA—a gay-straight alliance," Addie explained. "It's like a club where gay kids and straight kids meet and talk about things. And one of the things they talk about is how to make school a safe place for everyone. For heaven's sake, Joe, if you and Colin want to kiss, you have every right to. It shouldn't have to turn up as tabloid trash the next day in school!"

(Addie talks like this, what can I say?)

"We did not kiss," I told her.

She shrugged. "Whatever." What *was* it with my friends?

DuShawn grinned at me and waggled his eyebrows. "Don't knock it till you try it," he said. "It's sweeeeet."

"DuShawn!" Addie said, jabbing him and turning as red as the streak in my hair. I couldn't help noticing she was smiling, though.

All of a sudden I got this picture in my head of Addie and DuShawn kissing, but because I didn't want to totally lose my appetite (or my lunch), I pushed it away as fast as I could.

I honestly don't remember much about the rest of the day. I was kind of in a state of shock or something. Even without thinking about Addie and DuShawn kissing, I could hardly eat my lunch. It wasn't the rumors that were getting to me as much as the fact that Colin was sitting at his old table and never even once turned around and looked my way. Addie was going on and on about this whole GSA thing, as if being gay and twelve (or thirteen) (Colin is thirteen) and accused of kissing your boyfriend in public were suddenly her personal problems.

I tried talking to Colin between classes later, but he just mumbled something about how he couldn't talk right then and walked away. He wouldn't even *look* at me!

The next day we didn't have school because of

something called Staff Development Day. Ms. Wyman told us in math that it was a day for teachers to learn. I don't know what they were learning, but I wondered what they would do if they learned about Colin and me and all the stuff that was being said about us. And that got me wondering if any of the teachers were gay and if they'd had things like the kissing rumor happen to them when they were in school.☺

It's good we had Tuesday off. I got to have an entire day to feel sorry for myself and try to figure out whether I should hate Colin or not. I mean, I couldn't exactly hate him (he's Colin, hello), but I couldn't exactly like him either. I didn't feel like talking to any of my friends, and Jeff was in his room clicking away on his computer. (Probably writing total porn to that girlfriend of his.) (Not that I would have talked to him about what was going on, anyway.) (Can you *picture* it? "Oh, sure, Joe, the same thing happened to me when I was in seventh grade and got caught holding hands with *my* boyfriend.") (Yeah, that's gonna happen.)

I knew the only person I could really talk to was Aunt Pam. And that's just what I was going to do. The minute she got home from work, I was going to say we should

---

☺ Mr. D: I hope it's okay to be thinking about teachers being gay. I mean, it's kind of personal, but it's not an insult or anything.

make a big bowl of popcorn and go up to her room and hang out and talk. I was even going to come out to her— I mean, I know that she knows, but I've never said the actual g-word, and anyway, I thought it would kind of make it official and get the ball rolling, family-wise. "Aunt Pam," I was going to say to her, "I'm gay, and I'm having boyfriend trouble." And she'd be able to tell me what to do because she's super-smart and—remember?—she wants me to be so fine I'll shine.

But then when she did come home, I didn't have a chance to say anything, because before I could even open my mouth, she was telling me that she's moving back to New York *right after Thanksgiving*, which is only a few weeks away! She sounded all excited and happy. It seems her friend found them an apartment in this really cool part of the city and she's getting to start her new job sooner than planned and blah blah blah. She said she'd miss me, and she was sorry it was so soon. I think she promised to come back for Christmas. I don't know. After it hit me that she was really leaving, I kind of stopped listening.

As days go, Tuesday totally sucked, and I was sure Wednesday would be even worse. I was right, but not for the reasons I thought. It turned out nobody was talking about Colin and me anymore. The kissing rumor was so over. Why? Because this girl had let this boy touch her under her shirt on the stairs *right outside the main office*, and now she was a slut and he was a stud, and that's all anybody was talking about. It was like being inside some weird reality show on TV. Except in this case getting voted off the island was like winning. That's what it felt like to have nobody talking about Colin and me kissing—like we'd been voted off the island and we'd won!

I *almost* felt like a winner, until I went to my locker at lunch and found Colin's note. After that, I was back on the island and the biggest loser in the whole world.

LIFE LESSON: Middle school is like being trapped in a reality show where there's no way off the island and you're always a loser.

L is for
LEFTOVERS

The relatives have gone away and we're still eating the turkey loaf we made out of the leftover turkey. Usually, I love leftovers. When my dad and I make chili (which I sometimes make on my own) (it's *really* good) (maybe I'll be a world-famous chef when I grow up) . . . anyway, when we make chili, I always heat up what's left over and have it for breakfast the next day. I even like it on school mornings, which probably sounds gross when you think about it being 7:00 A.M. and eating nuked chili, but it is so not.

Next to chili, turkey is my favorite leftover. But not this year. This year, I hate everything about Thanksgiving—and leftovers. Because this year, it's not just food leftovers I have to deal with, it's people leftovers.

(Oh, and I should probably mention that we have all this leftover tofurky, too, because Addie and her parents were here. Trust me that the tofurky is going to be left over for a looooooong time.)

Anyway, you're probably wondering what I mean by "people leftovers." What I mean is, the stuff people leave behind them after they're gone. Aunt Pam moved out two days ago, and I keep finding her things all over the house. It's like she packed so quickly she didn't even notice how much she *wasn't* packing. Or maybe she just didn't care. Was she in *that* much of a hurry to get away from us? Like right now, I've got this hair-clip thing sitting on my desk. I found it in her room—her *leftover* room. I feel kind of bad about it because I gave it to her for her birthday a couple of years ago, and I know she liked wearing it. So why did she leave it out in plain sight on her dresser? Why didn't it matter enough to take?

She left tons of other stuff, too, mostly in her studio over the garage. She said she's coming back for everything at Christmas. But what about the empty feeling she left behind? I don't think she'll be able to come back for that. That's going to be around even longer than the tofurky.

The reason I know this is because it's been more than three weeks since Colin left the note in my locker, and the empty feeling I got after that hasn't gotten any better in all this time. I guess I may as well tell you what he wrote:

Joe, ☺

The guys on the team gave me a really hard time at practice last night. They kept asking me if the rumor was true, and some of them—even Justin, who's my _friend_—were saying things like, You'd better not turn fag on us, Briggs. Then they started making jokes about not wanting to shower with me, except I'm not sure they were all joking. I told them Kevin and Jimmy had made the whole thing up. I don't know if they believed me.

Joe, I feel really, really bad saying this, and I hope you won't hate me, but I think maybe we shouldn't hang out together anymore. I just can't deal with what's happening. Please don't be mad at me.

colin

P.S. I still wish I could be like you. I can't, and that's the problem.

I've tried really hard to hate Colin, but it just doesn't work. I miss him too much, and I guess I understand

☺ Mr. D: This is the closest font I could find to Colin's handwriting, which, as you know, is extremely neat for a thirteen-year-old boy (or anybody, for that matter).

why he had to do it. I've never been on a team, but I know what it's like for me in Phys Ed. When I first got his note, I was afraid he'd start making fun of me the way the other guys do. But that was stupid. Colin isn't like that. I e-mailed him that night and told him it was okay, that we could just ignore each other in school. But he wrote back and said, "No way." And he doesn't ignore me. He always says hi when he sees me in the hall, and we even talk sometimes. We just don't do Moonet and Pigasso in art class anymore. We don't laugh or bump elbows.

The hardest is lunchtime, sitting at the table with Kelsey and Bobby, and Addie and DuShawn, with them acting like couples, and hearing Colin's voice from across the cafeteria. That's the time I really do get mad. But then we'll be leaving and I'll see Colin on the way out and he'll give me this little shy smile, like he's saying, "I'm sorry." Of course, it might not mean that. It might not mean anything. Maybe it never even meant anything that he told me he liked me.

Addie got really furious about it when I first told her. She said she was going to talk to him, but I begged her not to, and for once she listened. Then she said, "This is all the more reason we need a GSA in this school!"

Whatever. We haven't even gotten this no-name-calling thing off the ground yet, and here goes Addie with another cause. She has more causes than her parents' car has bumper stickers. I guess it's cool to care so much and all that, but sometimes Addie wears me out. And, well, I'm not sure if having a club with the word "gay" in it would help or just make things worse.

Usually, I love Thanksgiving weekend because it's the first long break from school. And I was really looking forward to it this year because I thought it would give Colin and me a lot of time to hang out together. Yeah, well, that didn't happen.

Addie and her family left for the weekend the day after Thanksgiving, and Kelsey's been away the whole time. But Bobby and Skeezie have been around. They came over to my house this afternoon (Sunday). We were hanging out in my room eating turkey loaf and leftover sweet potato pie. Skeezie *est un cochon, vraiment!*☺ Really, he should wear a bib. I wouldn't have been watching him, except I had to keep an eye on where the sweet potato pie was going to land. I mean, bright orange on my lime green shag carpet would not have been pretty.

Bobby noticed the new painting on my wall right away. It's kind of hard to miss, since it's almost as big as the wall,

---

☺ French for "Skeezie is a pig, truly!"

but of course Skeezie, who was looking right at it, said, "What painting?"

"Pam painted it, didn't she?" Bobby asked.

I told him yeah. "She gave it to me when she moved out," I said. "She wanted me to keep it."

"Oh, that's a painting," Skeezie said. "I thought it was, like, wallpaper."

Bobby shook his head but otherwise ignored Skeezie, which is usually the best thing to do. "That was really nice of her, Joe," he said to me. "It's something to remember her by."

"Yeah, that and all the other things she left around here. Except I guess she'll be coming back for those."

Bobby said, "She'll be back for Christmas, right?"

"That's what she says," I told him. "I really miss her. Who's going to streak my hair or paint my fingernail?"

Skeezie said, "I'll do it."

"Yeah," I said, "like I'm letting somebody who can't get sweet potato pie from his plate to his mouth without half of it ending up on his shirt anywhere near me."

Skeezie looked down at his shirt and went, "You're exaggerating, JoDan. That's nowhere near half."☺

☺ Mr. D: I'm going to try to remember the rest of what we said, but I'm getting tired of having to say "he said" all the time, so I'm just going to put down our words.

Me: Even if she does come back at Christmas, it won't be the same. She's just going to turn around and leave again.

Bobby: You're lucky she comes back. I miss my mom a lot at Christmas. It's the hardest day of the year for me. Well, the day she died is hard, too. And her birthday. And Mother's Day. I hate Mother's Day.

Skeezie: Every Father's Day, I take a picture of my dad and burn it.

Bobby: Sometimes I have these dreams where my mom comes back for a visit. I know she's dead and all—I mean, I know it in the dream—so I don't get all freaked out the way Scrooge does when he sees Marley's ghost. It's kind of natural, her visiting. In this one dream, we went to the Candy Kitchen and had ice cream, and I told her what was going on in my life.

Me: I remember that your mom had a real sweet tooth.

Skeezie: Like you.

Bobby: Yeah, we liked our ice cream, all right. Rocky Road. That was her favorite. Another time, I had this dream where she was sitting next to me in school. Nobody could see her or hear her but me, but she was so *real* sitting there. She kept smiling at me and telling me how proud she was of me. I said to her, "What are you proud of? I'm not doing anything." She said, "You don't have to do anything to make me proud. I'm your mother."

Me: Aunt Pam says . . . said . . . that kind of thing to me, too. She said I'm good just the way I am. She told me I was going to do fine without her.

Bobby: My mom said that, too. That I'd do fine without her.

Skeezie: She said that to you in a dream?

Bobby: No, in real life.

Me: She talked about that with you? About . . . not being here anymore?

Bobby: Uh-huh. She told me that she was very sick and she was going to die. We didn't talk about it a lot. I was only seven. But she wanted to make sure I knew I'd be okay. We even talked about Christmas. She said she felt bad that she wouldn't be here to give me presents on Christmas or my birthday. She asked me to put her favorite picture of me under the tree every year. I don't know why it's her favorite. It's just this dopey picture of me sitting on Santa's lap.

Skeezie: Oh, yeah, I know that picture. I wondered why you always had it under your tree.

Bobby: Last year, I noticed for the first time that her hand is in the bottom corner of the picture. It's blurred because she's waving or motioning or something, but I can tell it's her hand. She was probably getting me to look at the camera. Or maybe she was telling me to sit still. I was always squirming around. Anyway, when I saw it, I completely lost it.

Skeezie: You lost the picture?

Bobby: I lost *it*. I started bawling my eyes out. Because she was there in the picture, you know? But she *wasn't*. Just her hand was there, and that was a blur.

Skeezie: The only thing my dad left was pictures. And us. I don't think he took one lousy picture with him. Man, he knew this was a permanent move, even if he was telling us it wasn't. "Trial separation," my butt. Whenever I look at the pictures he left, it's like what you said, Bobby—he's there but he isn't. The guy in the pictures is smiling, like he's happy to be where he is, happy to be with his little family. But that's not who he is. It's probably not who he ever was. He was probably lying to us the whole time. And then he left pictures behind to do the lying for him. That's why I have to burn them. It's them or me, get it? Pictures are killers.

After Bobby and Skeezie went home, I took out the one picture I have of Colin and me. Aunt Pam took it after we got into our Bert and Ernie costumes. It's kind of like the picture Bobby has of his mother's hand, or the ones Skeezie was talking about where his father's smiling and he doesn't know whether to believe the smile or not. It's like Colin and I are there but we're not there—because we look more like Bert and Ernie than ourselves. And Aunt Pam's kind of there but not there, too, because she's the one who made the costumes and the one who took the picture.

That picture is full of people leftovers. Skeezie's right—pictures *are* killers. I don't want to burn it, though, because, except for the few notes Colin left me in my locker and Aunt Pam's painting on my wall, that picture is all I have.

LIFE LESSON: People leftovers last a lot longer than the food kind.

DECEMBER

M is for
MERRY CHRISTMAS

AFTER THE WORST HALLOWEEN AND THE WORST THANKSGIVING EVER, CHRISTMAS TURNED OUT TO BE PRETTY GOOD. *REALLY GOOD,* actually. Aunt Pam came back just like she promised, and she gave me the *best* present! At first, I thought it was a joke. I opened this big box, which was so light I was sure there was nothing in it. It turned out I was almost right. The only thing inside was a needle.

"Cool gift," I told Aunt Pam, thinking, *Oh, great, she's moved back to New York City and she's doing drugs again.* Except, of course, it wasn't a drug kind of needle. It was the kind you sew with.

My mother figured it out right away. Meanwhile, I was so, like, *duh.*

Mom said, "I thought you were going to take him to the mall to do it."

"*I* can do it," Aunt Pam told her.

I cleared my throat. "Does anyone mind telling me what 'it' is?"

Jeff was, like, "Use your brain, numb-numb."

At that point, even my dad got it. "Your ear?" he said.

I couldn't believe it. My entire family not only had it figured out before I did, but they were telling me it was cool to get my ear pierced! They were even better about it than my friends!

FLASHBACK

I'm at the Candy Kitchen with Bobby, Addie, and Skeezie two weeks ago. I tell them I'm hoping I can get my ear pierced for Christmas, and they're all, like, "Way to go, Joe!" And, "That is so cool!" Stuff like that. But then Bobby gets worried that maybe having an earring will make me more of a target for being called "faggot" and "fairy" and other delightful f-words.☺ And that gets Addie and Skeezie worried, too.

I say, "Come on, you guys, I'm not going to be wearing a big dangly thing, just a little stud."

Of course Skeezie has to make a joke, saying *I'm* a little stud, ha, ha, ha. So funny I totally forget to laugh.

"Anyway," I say, "Kevin Hennessey's brother, Cole, has an earring, and nobody calls him names."

☺ Fruitcake. Flipper. Fajita. Fungus. Dr. Frank N. Furter.

"Duh," says Skeezie. "They don't call him names because he'll rearrange their body parts if they do."

"Well, my point is that Kevin can't really make fun of me for having an earring if his very own brother wears one. Besides, there are other guys who wear earrings and nobody says anything to them. Even Mr. Keller has one."

Mr. Keller is this new science teacher who all the girls swoon over.

Everybody's real quiet, and I get to thinking about the guys in our school who wear earrings. None of them is the kind you'd call "faggot" or "fairy" or other delightful f-words. They can get away with wearing whatever they want because they're guy-guys. I, on the other hand, am not a guy-guy, so I don't get away with anything. Isn't that special?

Finally, Addie says, "Well, I still think it's cool, Joe. I think you'll look good. Hey, I'll bet my mom's got some singles you can have."

"Singles?" I ask.

"The ones left after you've lost one of a pair."

This makes me laugh, thinking of wearing Addie's mom's leftover earrings, and pretty soon we're all laughing.

"Hey, JoDan," says Skeezie after we settle down. I try not to notice that most of the sprinkles from his ice-cream cone have taken up residence on his face. "Would it be okay if I get one, too?"

"An earring?"

"Yeah," he says. "I've been thinking about it, but then I tell myself I don't want to do it because, you know, my dad had one and all. But it would be cool if we both did it. I mean, if it's cool with you."

"It's cool with me," I tell him.

"We'll be earring brothers," he says.

"That is so weird," I say back, but I'm thinking how Skeezie and I don't really have much in common, even though we're friends, and how I like the idea of being earring brothers. I just hope he won't get in the habit of telling people that's what we are.

BACK TO CHRISTMAS

Aunt Pam gave me some other really cool presents, too— except she gave them to me privately. She said they were for after I came out to the rest of my family. Oh, yeah, I told her I'm gay. It happened this time when she called and I was the only one home and I was feeling really sorry for myself because of Colin. After I told her, she said, "I know you're gay, Joe. I've always known it. It's just part of who you are. You've always known who you are, too, and you've never been ashamed of it. That's one of the things I admire about you. Don't worry about your parents. They'll be fine. Jeff might have a hard time at first, but he'll get over it. And he's probably had it figured out for a long time, anyway."

"You're forgetting," I said, "that Jeff doesn't live on the same planet as the rest of us. He's in cyberspace."

Aunt Pam laughed at that, and that's when I told her I wished she didn't live so far away. And that's when she told me she'd be back at Christmas and she'd have some special presents for me.

So, anyway, on Christmas afternoon we were hanging out in my room and she gave me this box of presents she said she got in a part of New York City where a lot of gay people live. There was a rainbow candle and a little rainbow flag (she said rainbows are, like, this gay symbol or something) and a book of stories called *Am I Blue?* There was also a T-shirt that says I'M NOT GAY BUT MY BOYFRIEND IS. It's an XL, because Aunt Pam said I'd probably want to wear it as a sleep shirt—and only *after* I told my parents about being gay. She said she thought maybe it would help me laugh about Colin. I laughed about the T-shirt, but not about Colin. Actually, thinking about Colin still makes me sad.

Anyway, there were other things, too. Some really cool pins, and, oh yeah, one of my favorite things was a mug with the names of all these famous gay, lesbian, and bisexual people on it (only they're called "queer" on the mug). I mean, I knew about Elton John and Ellen DeGeneres, but did you know that Michelangelo and Leonardo da Vinci were queer? Wait until I tell Kelsey, she's all into artists. And Eleanor Roosevelt is on there! She was the wife of a president and the subject of my fourth-grade "Great American Women" report! I sure didn't read *that* about her in any of those books I read back in fourth grade!

I had just finished putting all the stuff back in the box when my mom knocked on the door. She said she had one more present for me, but she didn't know how I would feel about opening it in front of everyone, so she wanted to give it to me now. I was freaking out a little, wondering what it could be. You're not going to believe it! She gave me the exact same book Aunt Pam had just given me—a book of short stories that all have gay characters in them! Mom and Aunt Pam laughed, and I said, "Does everybody in this family know everything about me before *I* do? First the earring, and now this!"

"You may as well get it over with, Joe," Aunt Pam said.

So I got everyone to come into my room, and I took all the stuff out of the box Aunt Pam had given me, and I said, "Does this tell you anything about me?"

Jeff looked bored and said, "Can I go?" But my father grabbed him by the shoulder and made him stay.

"Why don't you tell us what it says about you?" Dad said.

Oh. My. God. I couldn't believe it was happening. I was going to say the words. Right out loud. To my mother and my father and my brother and my aunt (who already knew). I was going to say, "I'm gay."

And I did.

Jeff said, "Okay, can I go now?"

Aunt Pam was right. EVERYBODY ALREADY KNEW!!!!!

Nobody said, "You're only twelve, how can you know you're gay?" Nobody said, "It's just a phase." Nobody said, "You can't be gay (sniff, sniff)! Where did we go wrong (sob, sob)?" My mom and dad hugged me and told me they loved me and said they'd kind of figured out that's who I was and all they wanted was for me to be happy.

And that's when I started crying (sniff, sniff, sob, sob), because I wanted to tell them all about Colin and how *he* made me happy. But I couldn't tell them because it wouldn't have been fair to Colin, and besides, he wasn't making me happy anymore.

I guess maybe I was crying for another reason, too. Even though nobody was acting like it was a big deal, we all knew that it was. I'd said it. Out loud. "I'm gay."

I took one of the pins Aunt Pam had given me and put it on my shirt. It said CELEBRATE DIVERSITY. Then I took it off, thinking I'd give it to Addie, because it's one she'd really like, and I put on another one. I like what it says best of all: BEING WHO YOU ARE ISN'T A CHOICE.

The next day, Skeezie and Addie and Bobby came over so we could all exchange gifts. I gave Addie the pin, which she loved, and told them all about what had happened. They all slapped me five and said I was awesome. Then Aunt Pam took us to the mall, which was a total zoo, since it was the day after Christmas and all, and Skeezie and I picked out our earrings.

When we got home, Aunt Pam sat us down in the kitchen, numbed our earlobes with ice cubes and—Oh. My. God.— stuck a needle through our ears! Ice or no ice, it hurt! But now I have this way cool yin/yang☺ earring on my left lobe. And Skeezie has a silver skull on his. (Are we predictable or what?) And we are now officially earring brothers.

I love Christmas, and this was almost the best Christmas of my life. The only thing that kept it from

☺ ☻

being the best ever was the present under my bed, the one I'd bought for Colin before he broke up with me. I know it's stupid, but I'm keeping it there just in case we get back together. If birthday wishes can come true, maybe Christmas wishes can, too.

Hey, I'm a poet.

LIFE LESSON: Being who you are isn't a choice.

JANUARY

N is for
NAMES

IT'S FUNNY, BUT SINCE I CAME OUT TO MY FAMILY ON CHRISTMAS, being called names doesn't bother me as much. Like, when I got back to school, practically the first thing I heard was Kevin H. (who else?) calling out, "Hey, faggot!" And all I thought was, *Yeah, that's me. So?*

I didn't say it, but just thinking it made me feel better. It was like, *Okay, that's who I am. Who are* you *but somebody who calls people names?* Aunt Pam said that sometimes guys who call other guys "faggot" and other homophobic names are deep-down insecure about themselves. Like maybe *they're* gay and just can't deal with it.

Oh. My. God. Does this mean Kevin Hennessey might be *gay?*

Anyway, it turned out Kevin wasn't even talking to me. He was calling out "faggot" to this new kid I'd never seen before. I guess that's Kevin's way of saying welcome. The new kid is in our grade. In fact, he's in most of my classes, so I learned a few things about him by the end of the day.

1. His name is Zachary Nathaniel.
2. He wants to be called Zachary, not Zach. (Kevin's idea of being funny is to put his hand over his mouth and cough/say "faggory" for "Zachary.") (Will the hilarity never cease?)
3. He moved to Paintbrush Falls from New Jersey over Christmas. (I'll have to ask him if he knows my grandparents.) (They live in New Jersey.)
4. He's short and kind of muscle-y, which is because he was into gymnastics at his old school. He was not very happy to find out there's no gymnastics program here. Personally, I think he should be glad, because when he told one of our classes he was a gymnast, Kevin "whispered" to Jimmy, loud enough for everybody to hear: "Only faggots do gymnastics." (Maybe Kevin *is* gay?)
5. He's smart. Every single time a teacher called on him, he knew the answer.

6. He isn't what you'd call seriously cute. However, he does get these way cool dimples when he smiles.
7. He has this tendency to say, "Oh, my goodness." (Why doesn't he just stick a target on his chest and hand Kevin a box of darts?)
8. He told Tonni DuPré he loved her hair. Twice.
9. He giggles.
10. *Maybe Zachary is gay?*

Anyway, he seems really nice, and if Roger Elliott hadn't asked him to sit at his table at lunch the first day, I would have asked him to sit at ours, because to be honest, he seems to belong more at our table than Roger's. I'm guessing that Roger thinks Zachary is a jock or something. I'm also guessing that even with the gymnastics thing Zachary is so not a jock.

I know I'm supposed to be talking about names, but I just have to say one more thing about the first day back at school: Pretty much everybody (with the obvious exceptions) liked my earring. Even Colin. He came right over to my locker first thing and said, "I heard you got an earring. It looks great!"

I didn't ask him how he heard, but it made me feel good to know that he had. Like maybe he's got spies or something. We told each other all about our vacations and Christmas and all (I kept wanting to let him know I had a present for him under my bed, but I didn't because I didn't want to see the look on his face telling me he *didn't* have a present under his bed for me), and then the bell rang and Jimmy Lemon walked by and said, "No kissing in the halls, girls," and Colin turned bright red. That was the last time Colin and I talked for the rest of the day. But at least I found out he liked my earring.

Anyway, today (the fourth day back at school) we had the first meeting of the student council and the No-Name Party (that's Bobby, Addie, Skeezie, and me) to talk about creating a No-Name Day. We decided to have it during the first week of March, to give everybody lots of time to work on it.

It was very weird being at this meeting. We put our chairs in a circle, and Mr. Kiley and Ms. Wyman acted like we had come from all over the country or something for some big conference. We had to go around the room and say our names. Duh. As if we all didn't know each other already. I looked over at Colin right before I said my name. (Remember, he's on the student council.) He was half looking at me with that shy, secret smile on his face. And, I don't know why, but it kind of bugged me. I opened my mouth to say my name, and what came out was, "JoDan Bunch." Colin's smile went away so fast it practically snapped. It was like I'd said a dirty word.

After we introduced ourselves, we got talking about the kinds of names kids are called in school and what we can do to stop it. I was talking, too, but in my head I was thinking about how I'd called myself JoDan and how that had made Colin look all constipated. I thought about all the names I've called myself over the years—Scorpio and GoJo (don't ask) and J.D. and Jody (first grade and only for a day) and a whole bunch of others. I've always invented names for myself because, like I've said, I think "Joe Bunch" is seriously boring. (Although I started liking it after Colin told me he liked it.)

That's when I figured out why I'd called myself JoDan at the meeting. I wanted to get back at Colin, to show him that I wasn't going to call myself Joe just because he said I should. It was that dumb smile of his that made me do it. The way he smiled, it was like he wanted to tell me he still liked me but it was going to have to be our little secret. Well, you know what secrets can do to you—they're the worm that eats the rose.☺

By the end of the meeting, Addie was going on and on about all the plans for No-Name Day. I think there's going

☺ Mr. D: I got this from that poem you read us the other day.

to be a poster competition between classes or something like that, and maybe a student essay contest about the origins of different words that are used in name-calling. To tell you the truth, I wasn't paying careful attention. I was thinking about Colin and the way his face had changed. Like one minute he was secretly telling me he liked me, and the next minute he was all disapproving. I mean, who is he to tell me what my name should be?

After the meeting, he came over to me and said real soft so that only the two of us could hear, "I like your earring, Joe, and I like how you've toned down your act, but why did you have to say your name was JoDan? Why do you have to be so out there all the time? That's why people make fun of you."

Well, thank you, Dr. Colin. Except I don't remember you having a talk show and me calling in and asking for advice.

Oh. My. God. And I always thought Colin was so nice. Not to mention that I *thought* he wanted to be like *me*.

Wrong and wrong.

What did he mean about toning down my act, anyway? What act? And since when did I tone it down? Colin may be cute, but he is way more Ralph Lauren than I ever realized. What can I tell you? An original like me cannot be seriously involved with a logo-clone.

Addie wanted to do some research on words at the library and since we were walking home together, I went with her. The truth is, I didn't feel like being alone, because all I could think about was Colin, and that just made me feel sad and angry and confused.

I started looking through this name book Addie had pulled off the shelf. I couldn't find JoDan, but I did find Joseph. It's from the Hebrew and it means "He shall add." Which makes me think I should be good in math, which I am totally not. However, it *is* a cool name in some ways, mainly because of Joseph who ruled in Egypt and had that amazing Technicolor dreamcoat. (That is one wardrobe item I would *so* wear!) (Seriously.) (I mean it.)

Anyway, Daniel (my middle name, remember?) is also from the Hebrew. I guess my grandma Lily (my mom's mom, who's half Jewish) must have had something to say about naming me! It means "God is my judge." *Bo*-ring. (No offense to God or anything.) But then there's Daniel in the Bible, who was miraculously saved from the lions' den. Now, there's something I can relate to.

Paintbrush Falls Middle School. Lions' den. Oh, yeah.

Since I was into it, I looked up Kevin, which is Irish and means "handsome." Riiiiiiight. Excuse me while I stick my finger down my throat.

Colin *should* mean "handsome" (or at least "cute") (or

"hot") (but maybe also "not as nice as everybody thinks he is"), but it's not clear what it means. The most I could figure out was that it's from the French and is a nickname for Nicholas, which makes no sense at all. The book also says it means "victory."

Uh. No.

I don't know why, but I looked up Zachary, too. It's from the Hebrew, like my name, and it's a variation of *Zecharya*, which means "memory." I like that. It's kind of mysterious. Although anybody who says, "Oh, my goodness" all the time is about as mysterious as a glass of milk.

LIFE LESSON: You can't judge a person by their name.☺

☺ People's Exhibit A: Kevin = handsome. Not.

O is for
OY

Grandma Lily said to me, "You're twelve years old, *bubeleh*. What do *you* know?"☺

"I'll be thirteen next month," I reminded her.

"Still." She looked at me meaningfully, as if "still" actually means something.

I don't know what the other half of Grandma is, but she sure loves the Jewish half. The next thing she said was, "Oy, what do you need this *tsuris* for?"

Tsuris means "trouble."

"It's no trouble being gay," I told her.

She laughed at that. Joe Bunch, stand-up comic. Next thing, I'll have my own special on HBO.

"No trouble?" she said. "Tell that to Lester Rifkin."

☺ One thing I know is that *bubeleh* means "sweetheart" in Yiddish and that when someone calls you *bubeleh*, there's a 99% chance you're about to get your cheeks pinched. I also know that being twelve doesn't mean you don't know anything.

"Is he here?" I asked. "I'll tell him."

She laughed again. Even harder. I made a mental note to write this stuff down, in case I do have my own special someday.

Grandma is always saying you should tell what you just said to somebody you never heard of. Like, "So you think going outside without a jacket is funny? Tell that to Herman Lowy, may he rest in peace." (For two years I never went outside without a jacket because I thought Herman Lowy died from the cold. Then I found out he died in his sleep at the age of ninety-seven and never wore a jacket a day in his life.)

Anyway, Grandma and Grandpa were visiting from New Jersey this past weekend. Whenever they stay with us, Grandma spends a lot of the time asking my mother how she could have moved to a godforsaken place like Paintbrush Falls. My mother says, "Godforsaken? You live in Short Hills."

Grandma: So?

Mom: I rest my case.

They talk like this. Half the time, no one else has a clue.

When Grandma and Grandpa leave, my mother always takes a hot bath and tells everyone to stay out of her way for at least two hours.

I love my grandparents, even if they are a little dense at times.© Grandma Lily can be a piece of work, but she means well, and Grandpa Ray is a softy. The only problem with Grandpa is that there's a whole list of things he can't talk about (which means he doesn't want to *hear* about), and at the top of the list is anything to do with s-e-x. In Grandpa's book, being gay has to do with s-e-x.

I hadn't really planned on coming out to them, but they asked me about the earring and why I was wearing rainbow shoelaces (part of my Christmas present from Aunt Pam) and, well, what could I say?

Grandpa immediately got out of his chair and headed for the kitchen. He said he needed a glass of water, but he looked more like he needed oxygen.

That was when Grandma told me I was only twelve years old and what did I know. (For the record, this may be the one and only time she called me *bubeleh* and did *not* pinch my cheeks.)

Later that night, I overheard her saying to my mom that she could not *believe* Pam would give me such *inappropriate* presents, pushing that *lifestyle* on someone so *young*. She then went into her usual rant about how Pam had always been a problem and she hoped one day she would come to her senses (meaning, live a life

© Remember the trucks?

129

Grandma could understand) and settle down. Mom told her that Pam was a problem only to *some* people, that she was a wonderful influence on me, and that being gay was a life, not a lifestyle. She also said that Pam's gifts helped me feel good about who I was, instead of giving me the message I should be someone I wasn't.

I ran upstairs and put on my BEING WHO YOU ARE ISN'T A CHOICE pin. I was thinking of putting on my I'M NOT GAY BUT MY BOYFRIEND IS T-shirt, too, but I wasn't sure Grandma would get the joke.

Sometimes I wonder how come my mom is so understanding and cool about who I am, considering that *her* mom goes *oy* and *tsk* and *sigh* over everything from how the table is covered with clutter to how the kids are being left to raise themselves. (We should be so lucky.) Grandpa isn't judgmental like that; he just kind of lives in his own universe. If it were up to him, I would still be getting trucks and catcher's mitts for Christmas.

But just when you think you'll never get through to them, they'll do things like hug you when nobody's looking or kiss the top of your head and say, "You're something special, kid" (Grandpa), or, "Sweetheart, you know I just want you to be happy" (Grandma).

Sunday when they left, Grandpa winked at me, which

was his way of saying, "I may not love the fact that you're gay (or even believe it), but I'm not going to have a heart attack over it (if it's true, which I'm not saying it is)." And before she shut the car door, Grandma looked up at me, wagged her finger, and said, "I still expect great-grandchildren. Don't think this being gay business is going to let you off the hook."

Which means that it won't be long before Grandma is saying to people who don't even know me, "You don't think you can be gay and live a normal, happy life? Tell that to Joe Bunch."

They're funny people, my grandparents.

Oy.

LIFE LESSON: Even when they give you trucks or pinch your cheeks, grandparents can be pretty cool.

P is for
POPULAR (NOT)

I SO DO NOT GET POPULARITY. MAYBE THAT'S BECAUSE I'VE NEVER
BEEN POPULAR. AND FOR THE MOST PART THAT'S BEEN OKAY.

Except for that brief time in the fifth grade when I tried to
figure out how to be a guy-guy, I never really wanted to be
anything but myself.

Okay, in the interest of full disclosure,☺ this last
statement is not entirely true. About three weeks into the
sixth grade, which is so different from the fifth grade they
should give you a passport, I started spending a lot of time
in the nurse's office with these mysterious stomachaches.
While I was lying there on that little bed, thinking about
whose head had been on the pillow before mine and if
they had coughed a lot and what disease they had, and

☺ I picked this term up from C-SPAN, which I was only watching because I
dropped the remote while channel surfing and the batteries fell out and rolled
under the couch and it took me about fifteen minutes to find them. After being
stuck for one-quarter of an hour on C-SPAN, I have to ask: DO REAL HUMAN
BEINGS ACTUALLY WATCH THIS? ON PURPOSE? SHOULD WE SEND HELP?

while I was also trying to look pitiful enough not to be sent back to class, it occurred to me that the real reason for my stomachaches was that not being popular *actually hurts!* I didn't want to have to change in order to have everybody like me, but that didn't stop me from wanting to be liked. When I thought about what it might feel like if everyone did like me, my stomach hurt even more because that was so far from ever really happening. I mean, I might as well have imagined what it would be like to be the star of a trapeze act (which is ridiculous even to imagine, since those trapeze acts all have names like The Flying Fedoras, and mine would be called The Flying Bunches, which sounds like a couple of guys throwing bananas at each other). Anyway, the point is that there was a time when I really, really, *really* wanted to be popular, and I just didn't understand why that had to be so totally impossible.

I still don't.

But I don't care anymore.

I guess.

This is on my mind because DuShawn was saying at lunch the other day that Tonni (Tondayala Cherise DuPré, whose name, like her hair, is fabulous) is the only one of his friends who is giving him a hard time for going with a white girl, but that a number of his friends were all, like, *Eww, what are you doing with Addie Carle? She's such a loser*. DuShawn didn't say "loser" because he didn't want to offend Addie or anybody else at the table, but everybody knew what he meant. Especially when Skeezie came right out and said it.

What DuShawn actually said was, "You know what's weird? It's less of a big deal for a black guy and a white girl to go out than it is for somebody who's popular to go with somebody who's . . . less popular."

That's when Skeezie said, "You mean somebody who's a loser."

Miss Politically Correct (Addie) said, "We don't call people 'losers,' Skeezie."

And Bobby chimed in with, "Remember, we're trying to stop name-calling."

Skeezie smirked and said, "Right. Please turn in your hymnbooks to number one-fifty-two."

I'm not sure Skeezie is taking this no-name-calling thing seriously.

Anyway, we all got laughing, but DuShawn wouldn't let go of his point, which was that it's easier for any two people to go with each other than somebody who's popular and somebody who's not.

I said, "What about two girls? Or two boys?"

I don't know what made me say that. My heart was pounding like crazy.

"Like Bert and Ernie?" DuShawn asked, looking right into my eyes.

Addie jabbed him with her elbow.

I wasn't sure what to say next *(Hello? Script department? Dialogue, please!)* so I just kept staring at DuShawn. I guess this forced him to actually think, and you're not going to believe what he said. Well, *I* couldn't believe it, and it actually made *me* think.

He said, "If the two girls or the two boys were popular, they could get away with it. The problem is that most of the time the girls who'd want to go with girls or the boys who'd want to go with boys aren't popular."

Oh. My. God. It was the whole earring thing all over again! If you're cool, you can get away with anything. If you're not: *Fuh-get about it!* (I have no idea what cheesy movie I picked *that* up from.)

So here's an example of irony:☺ Colin is popular. He could get away with going with another boy (according to DuShawn's theory). But he won't go with another boy because he's afraid he won't get away with it. But he *would* get away with it because he's popular. Meanwhile, here

---

☺ Mr. D: Look who was paying attention in class on Thursday!

I am—Mr. Single and Available and Out (to my family and friends, at least) and Proud—and I can't go with anybody because I am *un*popular!

See why the whole popularity thing is confusing? And why it totally sucks?

LIFE LESSON #1: Popularity is a win-win for the popular kids and a lose-lose for everybody else.

LIFE LESSON #2: In real life (when you're grown-up and out of school) popularity doesn't matter.☺

☺ Mr. D: Please tell me I'm right about this!

Q is for
QUESTIONS

What did Colin mean when he said he liked that I'd toned down my act?

Why can't I hate him?

Why do I wish he was still my boyfriend?

Why are the following such a BIG DEAL?

1. 2 boys dating
2. 2 girls dating
3. Somebody who's popular dating somebody who's not popular
4. Being popular

On Monday, when Addie went to Mr. Kiley with a petition to start a gay-straight alliance, why did he tell her no?

When she said, "Why not?" why did he say it was because there were too many clubs in school already?

If that's the truth, how come yesterday he told Royal Wilkins she could start a knitting club?

Why did Kevin Hennessey try to rip up Addie's petition?

Why did he tell her that God hates fags?

Does he really believe that?

Do most people?

Does God?

LIFE LESSON:☺

☺ I'm sorry, Mr. D, but I couldn't think of one. Life lessons are sort of about having answers, and all I have this time are questions.

R is for
RELIGION

GET THIS! THE REASON MR. KILEY SAID NO TO THE GSA

is that Kevin Hennessey's *mother* is making a big stink about it! Tonight, my mom and dad came back from a school board meeting all steamed up. I could hear their voices all the way from my bedroom before they even got in the house, so of course I ran downstairs right away to find out what was going on. Jeff didn't because a) he had his headphones on and probably didn't hear them; b) he was undoubtedly IM-ing porn with his girlfriend, Clark; and c) he pretty much thinks my parents inhabit another planet and he's not all that interested in what goes on there.

Anyway, my mom walked into the house, going, "If that's what she calls religion, thank God we don't go to her church!"

Normally, my dad might have laughed at this, but he was as worked up as my mom was. "We're not taking this one sitting down, that's for sure," he said, and then I heard other voices and realized Addie's parents were storming into the house, too.

When they saw me, they got kind of hush-hush and "shouldn't you be getting ready for bed soon?" But then my mother said, "This is Joe's business as much as anybody's—maybe even more—and I think it's just fine that he knows what's going on."

"He may already know," said Graham,☺ "since it's all in response to Addie's petition."

"Not quite all," Lydia☺ said. "It's also about those ridiculous rumors."

"Even if they're not rumors, even if they're true, they're not ridiculous. And are they so terrible that we have to bring religion into it?" My mother shook her head angrily and offered to put water on for tea.

"What are you all talking about?" I asked.

That's when they started jabbering on at the same time (except my mom, who had gone into the kitchen to make tea), until Lydia, who's a lot like Addie, took charge and told everyone to shush.

"I'll tell you what happened, Joe," she said, indicating that I should sit down. I have to admit this made me feel

☺ Addie's dad, remember?
☺ Addie's mom, but you probably figured that out.

very grown-up, even more grown-up than Jeff who, remember, was upstairs porning with Clark.

"This Mrs. Hennessey person," she started out, "who, by the way, I have never set eyes on before in my life, suddenly shows up at the board meeting tonight, full of God and religion—"

"And self-righteousness," my dad put in.

"For a lot of people, those go hand in hand," Lydia said. "Anyway, she claims that she heard that two boys were seen kissing at school☺ and that several students were trying to start what she called a 'gay club.'"

"That would be Addie's gay-straight alliance," said Addie's father.

"He *knows* that, Graham." (Lydia and Addie are *so* much alike.) "The point is, she's all up in arms, and she's gotten others to join her in some sort of religious crusade. 'I'm a good Christian,' she says, 'and my beliefs, and the beliefs of most of the people in this community'—how *dare* she speak for most of the people in this community?—'do not include homosexuality or any other perversion.'

"Oh, it just *galls* me," Lydia went on, her face getting all red, with the muscles in her neck starting to stand out like ropes, "that people can say things like that! And in the name

---

☺ This was when my palms turned clammy and I started mentally measuring the distance to the downstairs bathroom because I figured it was only a matter of time until I might have to throw up.

of religion! Who is *she* to say she doesn't believe in homosexuality, or to call it a perversion, or say she loves the sinner but hates the sin? The last time I checked, love was not a sin, and those who love were not sinners. Excuse me, Mrs. Hennessey, but what if I told you I didn't believe in *you*! I'm sorry, Joe, I hope I'm not offending you with any of this."

Addie's parents know I'm gay.

I went, "Well, uh." I had no idea what to say. I wasn't offended, but I was kind of embarrassed. I was just hoping they weren't going to ask about the kissing rumor.

"Anyway," Lydia said, "she and this little group of sheep she brought with her went on and on about 'family values' and the 'sanctity of marriage'—"

"Bottom line," my dad put in, knowing we might be there all night if nobody cut in on Lydia once she got going, "is that she told the school board there would be 'serious ramifications' for Mr. Kiley if he agreed to the GSA."

"Meaning," said Graham, "that she's threatening him!"

"I thought he already said no to the GSA," I said.

"He did," Graham said, "but he didn't shut the door entirely. Lyd and I called him after we found out he'd turned Addie down and then told another girl she could start a club. He advised us to bring it up at the school board meeting and said he would rethink it if the board was open to the idea."

"Interesting, isn't it," Addie's mom said, "how Mrs. Hennessey somehow found out about it and showed up tonight with her little cabal?"☺

I found myself wondering about Kevin's dad and asked if he was at the meeting, too.

"I don't get the feeling Mr. Hennessey goes to meetings," said Graham. "But his wife sure mentioned him often enough."

My father nodded. "I think he's supposed to be the hidden weapon. You know, the big gun that Mrs. Hennessey says will come in and 'take care of business' if the school board doesn't go along."

Lydia snorted. "Which sounds to me like he's nothing but a big bully."

Like Kevin, I thought.

I asked if I could go upstairs. I didn't say so, but I wanted to write all this down before I forgot. Besides, I didn't think I could handle much more worrying about the kissing rumor and whether or not I was going to have to throw up.

So here I am, sitting at the computer in my room, thinking about the stuff Mrs. Hennessey said, and starting

---

☺ I had to look this one up. It means "a number of persons secretly united and using devious and undercover means to bring about an overturn, especially in public affairs, or to undermine or cause the downfall of a person in a position of authority." Awesome.

to feel pretty steamed myself. I mean, what gives her the right to believe in me or not? As far as I can tell, I was pretty much born the way I am. It's not like I woke up one day and decided to like boys. And even if I did (which I didn't), what business is it of hers?

I know a lot of good things have been done in the name of religion, but a lot of bad things have, too. (Just pay attention in history class if you don't believe me!) And it seems to me that hating people for what they are—and can't help being—is definitely a bad thing.

LATER

I went back downstairs to get a snack, and Jeff was in the kitchen, rolling his eyes at the sound of his name being called from the living room.

"Tell them I already went upstairs," he hissed at me, but it was too late. Dad came in and said, "Jeff, can you join us for a minute? Oh, Joe, you're here, too. Good, both of you come in."

Great. Just when I thought I might get through the night without puking.

"We were just talking about the Hennesseys," my mother greeted us. "What do you know about their sons? You're in the same grade as the older one, aren't you, Jeff?

And we know you and Kevin are in the same grade," she said to me.☺

Jeff shrugged. "Cole's a jerk," he said.

"Care to be a little more specific?" my dad asked.

"He's bad news," Jeff answered with another shrug. I think maybe Jeff doesn't know what "specific" means.

"Examples?" my dad prompted.

Jeff took a bite out of his Slim Jim. "He throws his muscles around," he said, chewing. "He picks on anybody and everybody. He's got a foul mouth. Oh, and you should see him with his brother."

"Kevin?" I asked.

"Duh," said Jeff. "What other brother does he have?"

"So, like, what does he do?"

"You've never seen him? He's always shoving him around, kicking his butt, calling him 'fag' and 'queer' and worse. Sorry, Joe."

"For some of us it doesn't get much worse than 'fag' and 'queer,'" I said.

"I said I was sorry, okay?"

I told him okay and then said I needed to get my homework finished and go to bed. My parents couldn't

---

☺ Believe it or not, I have never told my parents about all the stuff Kevin has done to me. I've let them know he's not real nice and that he picks on kids. I just never said who his main target is. I guess with the Gang of Five looking out for me, I never thought I needed to. Mostly, I guess I thought if I did say something to my parents, it would get back to Kevin and just make things worse.

really argue with that, so they let me go without grilling me about Kevin.

I'm not sure what I would have said about him, anyway. He sounds like a miniature version of his brother, who's probably a miniature version of their dad. Anyway, I really didn't want to have to talk about him, because for the first time ever I'm feeling kind of sorry for Kevin Hennessey—and I don't like the feeling.

All I can think of as I'm writing this is how Mrs. Hennessey was at that meeting calling herself a good Christian—and look at that family of hers!

LIFE LESSON: Religion is only as good as the people using it.

FEBRUARY

S is for
SURPRISES

life lately I don't even know where to begin. I totally *love* surprises. Always have, always will. Like, I'm probably the only kid you'll ever know who doesn't ask for clues about what he's getting for his birthday or Christmas. When I was little, I never went poking around in closets and under beds the way Jeff did, trying to find out what Santa was going to bring. And if my parents so much as uttered the words "Joe" and "birthday" in the same sentence for, like, the month before my birthday, I'd start humming or singing at the top of my lungs!

Well, tomorrow is my thirteenth birthday and I've been doing a lot of humming. But mostly it's because I've been pretty happy, not because anybody has been talking about presents or parties or anything.

The reasons I'm so happy? Surprises.

Surprise #1

Aunt Pam came up for my birthday and she's going to stay for the weekend! She told my mom and dad on the phone that since she pierced my ear for Christmas, she's getting me a tattoo for my birthday. You should have seen their faces for the ten seconds they believed her!

(I wish you could know Aunt Pam. She is *so* cool.)

(No Surprise #1: I miss her.)

Surprise #2

Mr. Kiley said yes to the GSA! Well, almost yes. After Addie's and my parents went to talk to the school superintendent—at which time they pointed out a few laws they said the school might be in violation of if they *didn't* allow a GSA—and after Mr. Daly said he would be the club advisor,☺ it was easier for Mr. Kiley to say he would seriously consider it just as soon as No-Name Day was over. Mr. Kiley even called Addie into his office to talk about it with him and Mr. Daly, so we know he means it.

Addie said that at the meeting Mr. Daly told them he has a son in college who is gay. He said, "It probably helps when you know someone, but that really shouldn't matter. Civil rights are civil rights. And *everybody* deserves respect." The next day, he gave Addie this button his son had sent

☺ Mr. D: THANK YOU SO MUCH!!!!!!!!!!!!!!!!!!!!!!!!!!!!!!!!!!!!!

him. It says IF GAY AND LESBIAN PEOPLE ARE GIVEN CIVIL RIGHTS EVERYONE WILL WANT THEM. How cool is that? I am so going to ask Aunt Pam to try and find that one for me.

Anyway, Mr. Kiley asked Addie to keep the whole GSA thing quiet for now. He said he needs time to "determine a strategy for dealing with certain members of the community who might object."

I didn't tell him, but I already have a strategy: If Mrs. Hennessey opens her big yap about how Jesus loves everybody but me, I'm going to say that maybe her sons are acting a little less loving than Jesus would want them to—and then I'm going to tell her *everything* Kevin has ever said or done to me!

(I can't believe I just wrote that. Please, God, don't let Kevin Hennessey get his hands on this notebook!!!!)

Surprise #3
SAVING THE BEST FOR LAST: Colin and I are friends again!

We're not *that* kind of friends, but we're friends.

It happened a week ago, on Friday night.

Dad had dropped Bobby and me off at the video store while he went to pick up pizza for dinner, and who was there but Colin and Drew. We kind of nodded and said hey when we saw each other, and then Bobby and I started looking at the "Star Power" section, while Colin and Drew went to the back to check out action DVDs. Bobby really wanted to see

One Flew Over the Cuckoo's Nest, and I wanted to see *Terms of Endearment.* It was your basic Jack Nicholson standoff.

All of a sudden, I heard Colin say, "Go with *Cuckoo's Nest.* It's excellent."

"Sold!" said Bobby as he grabbed *Terms of Endearment* out of my hands and shoved it back on the shelf. Before I could say anything, he'd run off to join Drew in the checkout line.

Colin and I stood there looking at each other. Or not looking at each other. But not moving, either.

Finally, I said, "What are you and Drew getting?"

Colin blushed and mumbled something about *Matrix.*

"Kee-*ah*-nu," I said, drawing it out to make it sound meaningful, like when Grandma Lily says, "Still."

"Right," he said, and blushed even harder.

Drew called his name and they left, and that would have been that, EXCEPT that later, after Bobby went home, I was writing an e-mail to Aunt Pam when I got an IM from GUESS WHO!!!

blackbirdboy: how was cuckoos nest

phonehome217: good / jack nicholson is weird / how was matrix 12?

blackbirdboy: very funny / it was #3 revolutions / my fave

phonehome217: i know

blackbirdboy: keanu is awesome

phonehome217: ooo, somebody likes keanu

blackbirdboy: cut it out

phonehome217: when are you going to

phonehome217: sorry I hit send by mistake

blackbirdboy: I have a present for you

phonehome217: ???????????

blackbirdboy: its yr bday next week, right?

phonehome217: yes

blackbirdboy: I have a present . . . a way of saying sorry

phonehome217: for what?

blackbirdboy: being a jerk / saying you should tone down your act

phonehome217: you said I HAD toned down my act

blackbirdboy: I guess I wanted you to . . . cause it was embarrassing to me . . . cause I thought people would think I was like you

phonehome217: wow you sure wouldn't want them to think THAT!!

blackbirdboy: that was dumb, sorry . . . what I meant was . . . you're different, ok? And that's cool, but I don't want to be different. Is that so terrible?

I was all set to write, "How about just being who you are?" but then I thought that sounded kind of preachy, like I was telling Colin how he was supposed to be. And I suddenly realized I didn't have any more right to do that to him than he had to do it to me. So instead I wrote:

phonehome217: do what you have to do. it's okay, honest.

blackbirdboy: really?

phonehome217: really

blackbirdboy: so we're friends?

phonehome217: hmm . . . when do i get my present?

blackbirdboy: LOL / tomorrow?

phonehome217: can't tomorrow / wait, better idea—come to my party—next Saturday night

blackbirdboy: OK

phonehome217: I have a present for U2

blackbirdboy: but my bday isn't until Aug

phonehome217: it's leftover from Christmas / I've been keeping it under my bed

blackbirdboy: LOL / yr present is leftover from Christmas too / it's been sitting on my desk / great, now that I told you I'll have to get you a second present for your birthday

phonehome217: no you don't / WAIT WHAT AM I SAYING? Second present: good.

blackbirdboy: LOL

phonehome217: TTFN

blackbirdboy: TTFN

So Colin and I are friends again—AND he's coming to my birthday party. And I could tell it all makes him happy, too, because he was doing a lot of LOL-ing there at the end. And . . . Oh. My. God. I forgot—there's one more surprise.

Surprise #4
Zachary is coming to my party, too!

LIFE LESSON: Jack Nicholson is weird.

T is for
THIRTEEN
MY PARTY WAS ON SATURDAY AND IT WAS *AWESOME*.

I'm going to tell you all about it, but first let me tell you how it happened that Zachary was there. We were standing in the lunch line together on Friday (he's been eating at our table for about a couple of weeks now) when he said to me, "So, how's your alphabiography going?"

I told him good, and then I said, "Mr. Daly isn't making you write one, is he?"

When he said yes, I went, "That is totally unfair! You just moved here, and everybody else has had since October."☺

"Mr. Daly is giving me an extra month to get mine in," he explained. "And he said I could write short chapters. Oh, my goodness, I don't know what I would do if I had to write long ones!"

☺ Sorry for the candid dialogue, Mr. D, but you can't expect us kids to think you teachers are perfect and wonderful 100% of the time. We're only human.

I was wondering if I should say something to him about the "oh, my goodness" thing when I noticed how he was picking up a pat of butter for his roll. Then I thought maybe I should say something about not keeping his pinky finger in the air like that. Oh. My. God. I was turning into his Guy-Guy Advisor!

Luckily, before I could say anything to him, he said (there's a reason I'm telling you all this), "It's hard to think of something for every letter, though, isn't it?"

"Yeah, like Z," I said. "You're lucky your name is Zachary."

He nodded, then said, "What about X? There's nothing but—"

"*Xylophone!*" we both shouted.

We broke out laughing, and I noticed his dimples again. I could feel myself starting to blush, which meant I had to pull an emergency change of subject. So I asked him what he was doing over the weekend. He just shrugged and said, "Nothing. It's hard making friends here."

Without even thinking about it, I said, "Why don't you come to my birthday party tomorrow?"

He went, "*Really?*" You'd think I'd invited him to go with me to the Oscars or something. "Okay, that would be great."

And that's how Zachary ended up at my birthday party, which brings me to the Main Topic: I'm THIRTEEN!!!!!

(Okay, now that I got *that* out of my system.)

I guess it *is* exciting. To be a teenager, I mean. Although when I look at Jeff, I'm not sure what's supposed to be so exciting about it. He sleeps, like, sixteen hours a day!

Some of my friends already are thirteen, and they said the main difference is that things are more expensive now. No more "twelve and under."

But, I don't know, I feel more grown-up somehow.

Not that you would know that from my party, which was totally fun and kind of goofy. After we went ice-skating at the rink (Zachary is an awesome figure skater), we came back and had what my dad calls "silly foods," including hot dogs (Tofu Pups for Addie), which were barbecued outdoors (hello, there's, like, two feet of snow on the ground!), sesame noodles, corn on the cob (see previous parentheses; my dad said even though it was the frozen variety, corn on the cob was a *must* because it's my favorite food), four kinds of ice cream, and this *five*-layer cake Aunt Pam made, where the layers were all tipped in different directions and had different-color frosting. And when I say color, I'm talking TECHNICOLOR: fuchsia and magenta and aquamarine, to name a few! When Mom told her she should be a baker, Aunt Pam scowled and said, "Has our mother been talking to you?"

(Grandma is always going on about how Aunt Pam

needs to replace "rock 'n' roll" with "respectable 'n' responsible," and it drives Aunt Pam crazy. As far as I can see, Aunt Pam *is* respectable and responsible; she just does things her way and not Grandma's. Like I said in O, Grandma and Aunt Pam have their issues.)

Anyway, Aunt Pam said she'd try to find the button for me (the civil rights one), and that it would be a little bonus birthday present, but her main present to me was this big stack of CDs. She said they were all singers I should know—Ani DiFranco, Dar Williams, Janis Ian, and Kris Delmhorst. Oh, and she also got me one by this band called the Red Hot Chili Peppers because she said I was a teenager now and it was time for me to "start rockin'!" (I swear I could hear Grandma say, "Oy," all the way from Short Hills, New Jersey.)

I'd never heard of any of these people, but I've sampled all the CDs and I really like them. (I have to be careful about playing the Red Hot Chili Peppers when my parents are around, though, because some of the lyrics are kind of embarrassing, if you know what I mean.)

Aunt Pam said she's seen Ani DiFranco in concert and she is guaranteed to blow my mind, and that part of her birthday present is to bring me to New York (on the train from Albany—by myself!) the next time Ani (that's what she calls her) has a concert, and she'll get us seats as close to the stage as she can, so I can have my mind blown, up close and personal.

I got other CDs for my birthday, too. One of them was Colin's leftover Christmas present. It was this double album with an all-white cover. I saw that it was the Beatles, and I figured out right away why he'd given it to me. Sure enough, I turned it over and there it was: #11 on Disc 1—"Blackbird."

His other present was a small silver hoop earring. I put it in right away, and everyone said it was totally me.

"In which case," Skeezie piped up, "you won't be needing that stud. Can I have it?"

I told him no, and he started whining about how we were earring brothers and that meant we were supposed to share, and, well, that wasn't *too* embarrassing. (Especially considering that when he said it, his face was a mess of cake crumbs and frosting.)

Anyway, I loved Colin's presents, and I think he liked mine, too. I gave him a shirt from the Gap. It wasn't the present I had under my bed. That was a Hawaiian shirt with about as many colors going on in it as Aunt Pam's cake. But after our last IM, I knew it wasn't fair to give it to him. That shirt was a lot more me than Colin. So I kept it and got him one of those polo-type shirts from the Gap instead. That's more his style—even if it doesn't have a little logo thingy on it. I did get it in purple, because, hey, I'm not about to feed the Straight (and Closeted Gay) Guy Drabness Monster. Besides, one of Colin's secrets that only I know is that his favorite color is purple. (He tells everybody else it's blue.)

I won't go into a whole list of my presents, because I wouldn't want you thinking I'm a total Material Boy (even if maybe I am), but I have to tell you my two Very Favorites.

Very Favorite #1

This big box came from Grandma Lily and Grandpa Ray about two days before my birthday. For some reason, I decided to wait until my party to open it, which I'm glad I did, because it just added to the Goofiness Factor. It was a truck—a big yellow dump truck!

I said, "I think the grandparents have finally lost it."

"Look carefully," my mother said.

I took the truck out of the box and turned it this way and that until I saw that there, on the back bumper, was a tiny rainbow sticker. I couldn't believe it!

"It was Grandpa's idea," Mom told me.

If all my friends hadn't been there, I might've started bawling. I mean, this is my grandfather who has to leave the room for oxygen and who has never before exhibited a sense of humor we're talking about.

I asked Aunt Pam if she had put him up to this, and she said, "No way. He did call and ask me what kind of bumper sticker he should get, but he wouldn't let me help him find it. He said, 'I'll go online.'"

My grandparents? Online? This was getting scarier by the minute.

Oh, the neat thing about the truck (besides the rainbow sticker)? The dump part is the perfect size to hold CDs! Finally, a truck I can actually use!

Very Favorite #2:
This one was from Zachary, and it was a toy, too. Nobody else got the joke, but I did, right away.

"Now you'll have something to write about," he told me.

"Yeah, me and everybody else," I said.

He smiled. (I tried not to notice his dimples.) "Maybe, but you'll be the expert."

"You're right!" I said.

I started banging out "The Shoop Shoop Song (It's in His Kiss)," which is my all-time favorite Cher song.

I was pretty good, for somebody who'd never played the xylophone before.

If Cher had been there, she would have totally loved it!

LIFE LESSON: Birthdays rock!

U is for
UNDERWATER

THIS PROBABLY WON'T SURPRISE YOU, BUT WHEN I WAS YOUNGER, I WANTED TO BE ARIEL. YOU KNOW. THE LITTLE MERMAID.

It wasn't because she was a girl or because she had a fin (although the fin *was* way cool); it was because I loved swimming underwater. I was so jealous of Ariel, the way she never ran out of breath and never needed to come up to the top. The funny thing is, all she wanted to do was come to the top and live on the land, and all I wanted to do was go under the waves and live in the water.

Once, when I was four, my family went on vacation in North Carolina, I think it was, where there was this humongous waterslide. I was too little to go down it by myself, so I rode down between my dad's legs. Every time we splashed into the little pool at the bottom (which was more like a wading pool than a real one), I'd push away and start paddling around underwater, pretending to be

Ariel. I could hear my dad's voice, which I'd imagine was King Triton's. I'd picture him puffing up all red-faced and muscle-y, going, "Ariel! Ariel! You come here this very instant, do you hear me?" And of course I'd disobey him, because that's what Ariel would do. I couldn't hear what my father was really saying. His voice was all gurgly. He probably *was* sounding like King Triton, telling me to hurry up, people were waiting at the top, this wasn't the time to dillydally, blah blah blah. But I couldn't help myself. I was on a big adventure with Flounder, and that was even more fun than going down the slide.

I got to thinking about all this because of a song that's on one of the CDs Aunt Pam gave me. It's called "Waiting under the Waves," and it's by Kris Delmhorst, whose voice makes me sad and happy at the same time. When I listen to this song, I think about all the times I've been underwater and how I've always had the feeling of waiting but not knowing what I was waiting for. That time in North Carolina, I guess maybe I was waiting for my adventures with Flounder to begin. Other times, at the community pool in Paintbrush Falls, I was waiting for the kids who were picking on me to go away. That usually worked because I could stay under the water a lot longer than they could, and they'd get bored and go find somebody new to pick on.

One summer, I discovered that I liked looking at boys—and some of them were the same boys who were picking on me! That was very confusing. That summer, I might have waited under the water for the confusion to go away.

Mostly, I think what I was waiting for (or maybe wishing for) was the world *above* the water to feel as calm and peaceful and safe as the world *under* the water.

Does that make sense?☺

LIFE LESSON: In the words of a very wise crustacean (and a good friend of Ariel's): "It's better down where it's wetter, take it from me."

☺ Mr. D: I'm not sure who I'm talking to. I just have the feeling when I write that I'm talking to somebody, the way I get the feeling these singers Aunt Pam gave me are talking to me when they sing. Do you ever get that feeling when you write?

MARCH

V is for
VICTIM (NO MORE)

TODAY WAS NO-NAME DAY. KEVIN HENNESSEY CELEBRATED BY calling me a "flaming fag" before the first bell rang and then defended himself by saying it wasn't "officially" school yet.

I celebrated by walking into Mr. Kiley's office right *after* the first bell rang and officially reporting Kevin Hennessey. Mr. Kiley invited Kevin to join us, and we spent first period together, the three of us, with me telling Mr. Kiley every single rotten thing Kevin has ever done to me and almost every single rotten thing he's ever called me (like I said back in E, there are some things that are too disgusting to repeat). Mr. Kiley asked me why I'd never reported any of this before, and I told him, "Because I was afraid to."

He nodded, as if he actually got it, then stepped out of the room to ask Mrs. DePaolo to get Kevin's parents on the phone. The minute Mr. Kiley was out of sight, Kevin turned to me with his face all tight like a fist and said, "You'd better *stay* afraid, Bunch."

"Of what?" I said. "That you'll tell everybody I'm a queer? I am a queer. Big whoop."

"You're sick!" he spat at me.

"Then don't get too close," I told him, sticking my face right in his, "or you might catch it. Hey, Kevin, maybe that's what you secretly want."

"Bite me," he said.

I told him I was a queer, not a vampire, and either way he wasn't my type.

Before Kevin could threaten me with physical violence, which I knew was the only thing he had left to threaten me with, Mr. Kiley came back into the room and asked me, "Joe, do you have any witnesses to the claims you're making?"

I'm sorry, but this cracked me up. "Only the whole school," I said.

Mr. Kiley honestly looked surprised. "And *nobody* has reported it?" he asked. "In all this time?"

I hate to say it, but it suddenly dawned on me that Mr. Kiley needed some educating. "Kids don't tell on each other," I explained. "And teachers sometimes don't see what's right in front of their own noses."

He shook his head sadly. "It sounds as if we might need No-Name Day every day of the year."

"No joke," I said. I didn't mean to be disrespectful, but really: no joke.

You should have heard it when Mr. Kiley got Kevin's parents on the phone. Maybe you did hear it. First his mother got on and was yelling so loud Mr. Kiley had to hold the receiver away from his ear. But that was nothing compared with how loud Mr. Hennessey yelled when *he* got on the phone. Nice people, Kevin's parents.

I couldn't make out what they were yelling about, but Mr. Kiley was saying things like, "This is not about disrespecting your religious beliefs, this is about your son disrespecting another student." And, "I will not tolerate that kind of language, Mr. Hennessey. If you cannot speak civilly, I will hang up. What did you just say? Do not threaten me, sir!"

Meanwhile, the whole time, I noticed out of the corner of my eye that Kevin was getting smaller in the chair next to me. I mean it. Honestly. He was kind of folding in on himself, especially when his dad was hollering on the other end of the phone. I had this little flicker of sympathy for him, the way I did the time Jeff talked about how Cole treats him. I was thinking that maybe his father hits him, and that's why he was shrinking the way he was. But that's all the sympathy I could manage. Just a flicker. Because no matter what Kevin's story is, I'm tired of how he talks to me and pushes me around. I'm tired of being a victim.

I don't know how it happened. Maybe it was the fact that it was No-Name Day. Maybe it was because I was wearing the pin Aunt Pam had just sent me that says NO ONE IS FREE WHEN OTHERS ARE OPPRESSED. Maybe it was remembering how last week Kevin had said something really mean to Zachary and I'd just stood there and pretended I hadn't heard it. Whatever it was, something finally snapped. It's like Eleanor Roosevelt said: "No one can make you feel inferior without your consent."☺ Well, today, I stopped giving Kevin Hennessey my consent.

It was so cool the way the rest of the day played out. I mean, here it was—No-Name Day!—and Kevin Hennessey gets suspended for calling me a name! We had an assembly with a speaker, and the poster contest, and all kinds of other stuff for No-Name Day, but all everybody was talking about was Kevin Hennessey getting suspended for something he's been getting away with for years.

I have to admit I'm still a little bit scared that he's going to beat me up the first chance he gets. Jimmy Lemon has already threatened me, but I'm not scared of Jimmy. He's all talk and no muscle.

At lunch, DuShawn told me, "Don't sweat it." He said

☺ I always remembered that from my fourth-grade report, but I never understood it—until today.

now that everything is out in the open to the whole school—including me being gay! Oh. My. God.—Kevin isn't going to mess with me. I guess he could be right. Because right after he said that, some boys (by which I mean guy-guys) came over to our table and told me they thought what I'd done was cool. They said that Kevin was a big seven-letter-word-starting-with-A and they were glad I'd "put him out of commission."

I'm, like, a hero!

Mr. Kiley announced at the assembly that next year we're going to have a whole week and call it No Name-Calling Week, and he's going to try to get other schools in the area to do the same thing. And he called Addie and me into his office at the end of the day and said he is approving the GSA and that we can get it going whenever we want.

At dinner tonight, I told my family about everything that happened, and they were really proud of me. Even Jeff grunted something about my being brave. Then my dad said, "I have to give Mr. Kiley a lot of credit, too. It's nice to know that educators can be educated."

I said, "You know what's even nicer? After No-Name Day, I have a whole week of No Kevin Hennessey!"

LIFE LESSON: "No one can make you feel inferior without your consent."—Eleanor Roosevelt

W is for
WRITING

I liked to write. But writing this alphabiography has been TF.☺

So I've decided that writing is going to be my new interest. I'm going to write short stories and maybe a play, and, oh, big guess what: Skeezie and I are going to write a humor column for the *Easel* (like you don't know what that is: the school paper. Hello).

It happened this way:

Kelsey (Bobby's girlfriend, remember?) draws for the paper (she's an awesome artist) (honestly) (maybe even as good as Aunt Pam), and she's become, like, best buds with the editor, Heather O'Malley. Heather asked her if she knew anybody who was funny. Right away Kelsey said, "Skeezie and Joe."

So Heather said, "Well, which one should I ask?"

☺ Total Fun, and Mr. D, I am so not brown-nosing. You asked us to tell the truth, and I am. I mean it.

And Kelsey said, "Why don't you ask them both?"

So that's what Heather did, and we both said yes. Now Skeezie and I are not only earring brothers, we're writing partners! (I just realized this means we'll be spending more time together, which means I am going to *have* to do something about Skeezie's skanky eating habits.)

Heather also asked me to write an op-ed piece for the *Easel* (Culture Note: "op-ed" stands for "opinion editorial") on "Why We Need a GSA at Paintbrush Falls Middle School." This was Addie's idea (of course), but Heather really liked it, and she said that I should be the one to write it.

Oh. My. God. Maybe instead of growing up to be a famous designer or actor or whatever, I'll be a famous writer. How cool would that be?

(Grandma Lily called tonight, and when I told her what's going on, she said, "First you're gay and now you're a famous writer, who can keep up?" Then she told me not to put the cart before the horse. Whatever that means.)

(Maybe it means I have to write something before I can be a famous writer.)

(As Pooh would say: "Oh, bother.")

Well, I guess if I'm going to become a famous writer, I'd better get started. I have a lot to say about why we need a gay-straight alliance, because even though Kevin Hennessey is "out of commission," he'll be back, and besides, there are a lot of other kids in this school who think it's no big deal to say "that's so gay" or call somebody a faggot. They should only know how that makes *me* feel (and other kids, too, who might not even be gay)—and they will know, because I'm going to tell them!

LIFE LESSON: I figured it out—when you're writing, the person you're talking to mostly is yourself.

X is for
XYLOPHONE

Top Ten Things You Need to Know About the Xylophone☺

1. Toy xylophones aren't really xylophones. *Xylo* comes from the Greek word *xylon*, which refers to wood. Real xylophones have wood bars. Toy xylophones have metal bars, so they should be called "*metalo*phones". Does that mean that if the bars were made out of Scotch tape, the instrument would be called a "*cell*-o-phone"?

2. How many people does it take to play a xylophone? Some large xylophones require two to three performers using up to six mallets to strike the bars. Toy xylophones require one child to strike the bars, a second child to yank the mallet

---

☺ Mr. D: I found this information on the Internet. Or most of it, anyway. I added some stuff of my own. I think you'll be able to tell which is the stuff I added.

away, and a parent to yell, "Don't make me come in there!" from the other room.

3. The xylophone is brighter in tone than its cousin the marimba. (Hey, I have a lot in common with the xylophone—I'm brighter in tone than my cousin Miranda!)

4. The xylophone is featured in a number of classical pieces, including *Symphony No. 6* by Gustav Mahler, *Carnival of the Animals* by Camille Saint-Saëns, and *Hello, Is Anybody Home?* by I. M. Yourdoorbell.

5. Even though the word "xylophone" starts with an x you do not make the x-sound when you say it. You make the z-sound. That is because if you made the x-sound, you might end up spitting on somebody. Which explains why so few words start with x.

6. Xylophones are usually placed on stands with wheels so they can be moved around easily. If that's the case, shouldn't xylophone players be placed on roller skates?

7. Mallets are also called "beaters." For a bright and sharp sound, use a hard beater. For a gentle sound, use a soft beater. For an omelet, use an eggbeater.

8. It is said that if you dream of seeing a xylophone, it means you will achieve your greatest ambition. On the other hand, if you dream of *being* a xylophone, it means it's time to call your therapist.

9. There are different kinds of xylophones played in different parts of the world. Some of their names are the marimba, the balafon, and the da'uli da'uli. Some of the names of xylophone *players* are Fred, Harry, and Mildred.

10. Cher, Julia, and Keanu do not play the xylophone.

LIFE LESSON: As x-words go, you can't beat "xylophone." (Except with a mallet.)

Y is for
YESTERDAY

any ordinary day, but then the most amazing things happened. You will not *believe* what I found out! Are you sitting down? *Kevin Hennessey is not coming back to school!* Neither is his brother, Cole! Everybody was talking about it. The story is that his parents were so disgusted with Mr. Kiley and the school board (and probably didn't want to have to own up to the fact that their sons are total bullies, like their father) that they're taking Kevin and Cole out of public school and sticking them in St. Andrew's! Poor kids at St. Andrew's, is all I can say.

Jimmy Lemon walked around all day looking like he was sucking on his last name. I almost felt sorry for him. I mean, he did lose his best friend. But hey, maybe now he stands a chance of turning into a decent human being.

Even with Kevin going to St. Andrew's, I still worry about him beating me up. We may no longer go to the same school, but we live in the same town, and Paintbrush Falls is not very big. But who knows, maybe at that parochial school they'll teach him to be a real Christian and stop being a bully. They believe in miracles, right? It could happen.

I was afraid the story might all turn out to be a rumor, but my dad said it was true. He told me that Mr. Kiley and the school board (all except one member, whose name he wouldn't tell me, no matter how much I begged) stood up to Mrs. Hennessey and her—what was that word Addie's mom used? oh, right—cabal, and that was the end of it. He did say this one board member (He or She Who Shall Not Be Named) was making noises about starting trouble in the fall and fighting the GSA, so guess what. My dad is going to run for school board! He said Mr. Kiley needs all the support he can get to keep doing the right thing.

You want to know why else yesterday was such a good day? Because Colin asked if he could come over and we could watch a movie together. I told him I already had plans to go with the Gang of Five and some other friends to see that new Keanu Reeves movie, and did he want to come, too. So we all went, and right in the middle of the movie Colin whispered to me that Keanu was his favorite movie star. I whispered back that Keith Hernandez was my favorite baseball player. Colin was all, like, *really?* and *did you see the game where he blah blah blah*, and I had to own up to the fact that I'd heard Jeff talking to a friend about him, and I had no idea who Keith Hernandez was, I just liked his name. Colin cracked up, which got me laughing, too, and Skeezie hit me on the back of my head with his box of malted milk balls and told me to zip it.

So now you know that Skeezie was sitting behind me, but guess who was sitting next to me? Zachary! Colin was on one side of me and Zachary was on the other. For some reason, this kind of freaked me out, but I don't know why.

After the movie, we all went to the Candy Kitchen for ice cream. We were having the best time until Addie and DuShawn got into a fight over how the girl in the movie had to act all dumb so Keanu could look cool and manly. DuShawn got so frustrated with Addie that he just left, and Addie cried. Actually *cried*. I've never seen Addie cry in my whole life, and it made me feel terrible. But she said she and DuShawn fight sometimes, and they always make up. She said the problem is that they look at things differently, and they both have really strong opinions. (Duh. Really?) Then she said, "At least making up is fun." That put the picture of them kissing in my head, and all I could think to say was, "Gross," which just shows I still have some growing up to do.

While we were walking home, I asked Bobby (privately)

if he and Kelsey ever fought, and he shook his head like he didn't even know what I was talking about. Those two are so funny. After, like, six months of going out, they still blush around each other all the time, as if they're embarrassed just to be breathing the same air. I'm going to nominate them as "Cutest Couple" for the yearbook, even though, hello, it's *always* Sara and Justin. But who knows? So much is changing this year, maybe Sara and Justin will just have to settle for runners-up.

Even with the fight, it was the *best* evening, just being with a big group of friends. When I got home, Addie IM-ed me and told me she and DuShawn had already made up (on the phone, which wasn't as much fun, she said), and could I come over to her house tomorrow (which is now today) to talk about the GSA. I wrote back and told her that Zachary was coming over to hang out at my house, and she wrote back and said, "Bring him," and I said I didn't think he was quite ready for GSA-talk.

"Besides," I wrote Addie, "it's the weekend! Give it a rest!"

Honestly, Addie is so intense I don't know how she doesn't need all weekend just to sleep and get over herself.

Right after I finished IM-ing with Addie, Aunt Pam IM-ed me. She said she was missing me and couldn't wait for me to come visit her in New York City. She doesn't think Ani is going to perform there until the fall, so I have *got* to visit before that. She told me she'd talk to Mom and Dad about my coming down this summer—for a whole week! She's going to show me *everything* and take me *everywhere*. She's even got some gay friends she wants me to meet. People like me! That will be so awesome!

Then she asked me what color my hair is these days. I felt kind of bad telling her the truth, but I did. I said it was brown. I've stopped streaking it, and I don't paint my pinky fingernail anymore either, because, I don't know, all of that was kind of a special Aunt-Pam-and-me thing. Oh. My. God. Maybe I *am* toning down my act! (Not really. I still have a closet full of Hawaiian shirts and you should *see* the hi-tops I'm getting: bright green with hot pink piping!)

Oh, I almost forgot: Yesterday, Heather O'Malley said she thought my op-ed piece about the GSA was *perfect* and that Skeezie's and my humor column about where people sit in the cafeteria was a riot! Mr. Daly told me he'd read them, too (he's the advisor for the *Easel*) and he thinks I've come a long way as a writer. He said I show real promise!

So yesterday was a great day. I don't know if it was the best day of my life, but it was definitely in the Top Ten!

LIFE LESSON: A day can start out ordinary and end up being in the Top Ten.

Z is for
ZACHARY (OF COURSE)

ZACHARY CAME OVER TODAY AND I TOLD HIM I LIKED HIS DIMPLES.

Just like that.

I said, "I like your dimples."

He giggled and went, "Oh, my goodness."

I was all set to say something about how maybe he shouldn't say that at school so much, and maybe he shouldn't wave his hands around when he talks (*so* Aunt Priscilla!), and maybe he shouldn't keep his pinky finger in the air when he reaches for a pat of butter, but then I thought, *Who am I to talk? Puh-leeze.* Besides, Zachary is, like, the happiest person I ever met. Why mess with success?

So instead I said, "Will you teach me to do a headstand?"

Because he's a gymnast, remember?

And I'm a total klutz.

And he said, "Really? Sure!"

It took, like, for-*ev*-er, but I finally managed to do one. I kind of missed having his hands around my ankles after he took them away, but the feeling of being upside down and staying there, all by myself, was AMAZING!!!

Both of us cheered when I finally fell over, and then we got punchy because of the zillion times I'd fallen over before that (Zachary called me Mr. Wobbles) and then we couldn't stop laughing.

Mom heard us, and she got laughing, too. When she asked Zachary if he would like to stay for dinner, all he could do was nod because he was laughing so hard.

After dinner, we hung out in my room and talked. Who knew we'd find so much to talk about? And let me tell you, once he gets going, Zachary can talk! You've probably figured out by now that he also likes to laugh. His laugh is kind of goofy, and the sound of it is really contagious.

He told me how much he likes my new hi-tops and the way they kind of match my room. And then he told me how much he likes my room and how everything in it is so me. At one point, he picked up this notebook with my name on it, except the name was JoDan.

"What's up with that?" he asked.

I explained about how I used to give myself other names all the time.

He smiled his dimple-y smile and said, "Why? You're totally Joe."

"Meaning?"

"You're yourself," Zachary said with a shrug. "Totally."

I thought about how Colin had told me that same thing, but there was a difference with Zachary. "You're yourself, too," I said.

Zachary said, "So we're both totally Joe." Even though that made a weird kind of sense, it got us laughing, and before you know it we were laughing hysterically. And then we were racing each other to the bathroom we both had to pee so bad.

I have this feeling Zachary and I are going to be best friends. We might even be boyfriends someday, who knows? (Did I tell you he's actually a lot cuter than I first thought he was?) Right now, though, Zachary is kind of clueless about who he is—the gay part, I mean—even if the rest of the world figures maybe that's who he is. That includes me. But hey, the rest of the world could be wrong. Zachary will figure himself out when he's ready. As for me, well, I may have figured out that I'm gay, but I'm sorry, I am *not* ready to exchange saliva with anybody. The boyfriend thing can *so* wait.

It's funny, I started this alphabiography with my oldest friend, and I'm ending it with my newest friend. I never thought I could write this much, and now that it's coming to an end, I feel sad that I have to stop, sort of the way you feel when you're almost at the end of a really good book and you know you're going to miss the main character. But in this case, the main character is me! Myself. Joe (formerly JoDan) Bunch.

I guess there just aren't enough letters in the alphabet to tell my story, or maybe it's that there's still so much left to happen.

Like next Thursday, the *Easel* is coming out with *my writing* in it!

And next Saturday, Zachary and I are going to the mall together, and then we're going back to his house to make pizza from scratch because he loves to cook as much as I do!

And the week after that, we're having our first GSA meeting—and Mr. Daly's son is coming to talk to us!

And in June, right after school lets out, I'm visiting Aunt Pam in New York City—for a whole week!

And next fall, I'm going to visit her again and hear Ani DiFranco in concert where I will have my mind blown, up close and personal!

And the fall after that, I'll be in HIGH SCHOOL!

And maybe sometime in high school (I have four whole years, so it *could* happen), I'll be ready to exchange saliva and I'll be voted one half of the Cutest Couple of the Year—and our photo will be in the yearbook! I'm trying to picture who the other half of the photo will be. Maybe Zachary. Maybe Colin. Maybe Leonardo. Maybe Keanu.☺ Or maybe somebody I haven't even met yet. I guess I'll just have to wait to find out. And that's okay, because you know me—I *love* surprises!

LIFE LESSON: Alphabiographies should be full of *italics*, CAPITAL LETTERS, and exclamation points! (Just like life!) And they should never end with the words "The End." They should always end with:

TO BE CONTINUED!

☺ ☺

Reading Group Guide
Totally Joe
by James Howe

Discussion Topics

1. In his opening letter to Mr. Daly, Joe writes, "Let's face it, I'm not exactly your average Joe and I get called plenty of names because of it." To what types of names is Joe referring? What things make Joe seem other-than-average? How does Joe seem to feel about these qualities of his personality?

2. Who are Joe's three best friends? What does he like best about each of these people? How are Addie, Skeezie, and Bobby also dealing with qualities that make them "not exactly average"? Why do they call themselves the Gang of Five?

3. In the chapter entitled "B is for Boy," what does Joe describe as the qualities of a "guy-guy"? Do you think his description is accurate? What have been the results of Joe's occasional attempts to behave like a "guy-guy"? Have you ever tried to act like a certain "type" of person—or the way you understood this "type" of person to be? Describe the experience.

4. Who is Colin Briggs? How does Joe come to realize that his feelings for Colin are mutual? What obstacles stand in the way of their relationship? Compare and contrast Joe and Colin's relationship with those of Addie and DuShawn, and Bobby and Kelsey. What frustrations does Joe feel when he observes his friends' romances? What might you say to Joe if he were to share such frustrations with you?

5. Why is Joe's favorite movie *E.T.*? In what way does he identify with this extraterrestrial character? What (or where) is Wisteria? Have you ever felt like you really didn't belong, as if you came from another planet? Is there a movie or book that has special significance for you? Explain.

6. Why do you think Joe seems able to be rather matter-of-fact about not being in the popular group, about kids like Kevin Hennessey existing in the world, and even about not everyone being accepting of gay people? Who are the people in his world who make him feel accepted and just right the way he is?

7. Compare and contrast Joe's parents with Colin's parents. In what ways does each boy's family have an effect on his ability to fit into the world—and on his ability to be himself?

8. In Chapter "G is for the Gang of Five," Addie asks her friends, "If you love somebody, do you go along with them even if you don't feel right about it?" Answer her question. In what way does Joe "go along" with Colin, despite disagreeing with his position? Cite at least one other instance in the novel when standing up for friends causes difficulties for characters' romantic relationships.

9. Have you ever "gone along" with an action or opinion contrary to your own because of your feelings (romantic or otherwise) for another person? Describe the situation. Were you ever able to share your true opinion with this person? Can a relationship stay strong if one of the people in it is suppressing his or her true feelings or opinions? Why or why not?

10. As what characters do Joe and Colin disguise themselves on Halloween? What happens to their relationship after Halloween? Why do you think events unfold as they do? What does Joe learn from the demise of his relationship with Colin?

11. What "life lesson" does Joe record at the end of the "M is for Merry Christmas" chapter in which he comes out to his family? Do you believe this lesson is true? Is this a lesson that is hard to face? Why or why not?

12. In Chapter "N is for Names," Joe wonders if Kevin or Zachary might be gay. What prompts him to wonder about these individuals? Why do you think some people are more comfortable with their sexuality than others?

13. What new organization does Addie propose to start at the middle school? Which people object to Addie's proposal? From what people do Addie (and Joe) find support?

14. Why are no-name-calling, a gay-straight alliance, and other tolerance campaigns or clubs a good idea? Why is tolerance important? Is your school a place of tolerance, where you feel you can be yourself? Explain your answer.

15. What gifts does Joe receive from his aunt Pam, his grandparents, and Colin that show their support and care for him? Have you ever received a gift that showed you how much a friend or relative understood you? How did this make you feel? Have you ever chosen or given a gift to show another person your support? Describe this experience.

16. How does Joe finally defeat Kevin Hennessey in chapter "V is for Victim (no more)"? What insights into Kevin's personality are revealed in the later chapters of the novel?

17. While much of the novel is about Joe's identity as a gay boy, what other important talents and interests, which may shape Joe's future, does he discover in the final chapters—and perhaps through the experience of the alphabiography assignment? Have you ever been surprised to discover a new interest or talent? How do your talents make you stronger?

18. How does Joe feel about Zachary's mannerisms? Does he make any comments about them? How might his experience with Colin have affected Joe's thoughts about, and behavior toward, Zachary?

19. What does it mean to experience junior high school outside of the mainstream crowd? What does it take to fit in? Can everyone fit in if they try hard enough? What should you do if you don't find yourself fitting in? Should you care? Do you think everyone—even kids in the most popular crowd at your school—feels like an outsider at one point or another? Why or why not?

20. At the end of the novel, how does Joe feel about his life so far? Are you as optimistic about the future as Joe?

Read on for Addie's side of the story!

You Are Who They Say You Are

They say in the seventh grade
you are who they say you are,
but how can that be true?

How can I be a
Godzilla-girl
lezzie loser
know-it-all
big mouth
beanpole
string bean
freaky tall
fall-down
spaz attack
brainiac
maniac
hopeless nerd
bad word
brown-nosing
teacher's pet
showing off
just to get
attention—
oh,
and did I
mention:

flat-chested
(that's true)
badly dressed
(says you)
social climber
(such a lie)
rabble-rouser
(well, I try)
tree-hugging
tofu-eating
button-wearing
sign-waving
slogan-shouting
protest-marching
troublemaking
hippie-dippy
throwback
to another
time and place?

How can I be all that?
It's too many things to be.
How can I be all that and
still be true to the real me
while everyone is saying:

This
is
who
you
are.

Every morning I wake up worrying

and *not* about crushes
or acne or whether
I should stuff my bra
so people will know
I'm wearing one.

I worry about
global warming and
polar bears dying and
war and
more and
more and
more.

I worry about
injustice and
how to make the world
a better place,
because I contend
that if you are not part
of the solution,
you are part
of the problem.
I worry about
the rights of minorities
and I worry about
all the people

who love people
that the people who hate them
don't want them to love.

I worry about
my parents and
I worry about
my friends and
I worry about
people I don't even know
who have lost their homes
and their jobs and have
nowhere to go and
I worry about
what happens to
all of their pets and
I worry about
the economy and
the national debt.

I worry about
the animals that are
going extinct
and the animals that are
abused just so we can have
a new scent of perfume
or a new kind of shoes.

I worry how in the world
the world will ever be okay. Then
I turn off my alarm
and get on with the day.

Rush Hour

Morning. Toast. Butter. Jam.
Eggs? No thanks. I am
gathering up my homework,
they are blowing on their tea.

Grandma's coming for a visit.
That's nice, I say. Is it
for a weekend or a week?
Backpack. Keys. Other shoe.

A week or maybe more. Dad
shakes his head at bad
news in the paper. Cereal?
Only if there's Special K.

Why did I wear black pants?
Mom asks after a chance
encounter between both her legs
and both the cats.

Look at the time. Dishes. Sink.
Feed the cats. Quickly drink
the last of the orange juice.
Grab a sweater.

Joe's at the door. Let's go,
he calls out, and I know
I'm forgetting something.
Where's my kiss? calls Dad.

Peck on the cheek. Money
for lunch. Mom says, Honey,
remember what we talked about.
I've no idea what she means.

I will, I say, and I'm out the door,
the cats pushing ahead, off to explore.
Joe says something that
makes me laugh.

Sidewalks. Curbs. Friends wave
at us from the next street. They've
got backpacks. Toast. Butter. Jam.
Who knows why I'm happy.
I just am.

Becca Has Something to Say

My best friends are
Joe
and
Bobby
and
Skeezie,
and even though I have other friends,
these three are my best, oldest, truest,
and forever ones.

This morning, between English and art,
in the three minutes when the hall
is like a race being run by animals
sprung from their cages, when it's all
you can do to get to your locker
and get to your class,
Becca Wrightsman takes the time
to point out that my best friends are
all boys. "Really, Addie," she says,
"that's *so* gay." She smiles
as if *she* were my best and oldest
and truest and forever friend
before shouting, "Tonni, wait up!"